Croc's Return

Bitten Point, #1

Eve Langlais

D1607640

Copyright and Disclaimer

Copyright © April 2015, Eve Langlais
Cover Art by Yocla Designs © July 2015
Edited by Devin Govaere
Copy Edited by Amanda L. Pederick
Line Edited by Brieanna Roberston
Produced in Canada

Published by Eve Langlais
1606 Main Street, PO Box 151
Stittsville, Ontario, Canada, K2S1A3
http://www.EveLanglais.com

ISBN-13: 978-1517296902
ISBN-10: 1517296900

Chapter One

I can't believe the dog gets the front seat in the truck.

Indeed, the big-eyed canine—who barely consisted of a mouthful at five and a half pounds—that his brother called Princess, held the seat of pride *inside* the truck while Caleb merited the box at the back.

Forget logic. Caleb had tried to argue at the train station where his brother awaited him, leaning against the blue body of his Ford pickup truck.

"Hey, Connie," Caleb had said to his bro upon spotting him, which was the first thing he did wrong, closely followed by his second, "Packed on a few pounds while I was gone, I see."

It wasn't just women who took offense at weight jokes.

By the time Caleb stated, "Can you get this rat out of the front seat?" things had evolved from awkward to someone was gonna get hurt.

The frost in his brother's expression would have made a more easily intimidated man shiver.

"That is not a rat. That is a long-haired Chihuahua," his brother informed him coldly. "And my name, since you seem to have forgotten, is Constantine."

Caleb might have argued about it a bit more, but given he was trying to make amends with his family—and this particular branch of his family had grown quite

3

a bit since he'd left—he didn't push the point. He'd wait until later, after a few beers.

Or we could set the tone for how things are gonna go right now. Caleb's time in the military had given him a boldness that resulted in more than a few scraps—his version of stress relief. "That is not a dog." A comment that was met with a low grown and a lifted lip from the fresh appetizer in the front seat.

A dog? Snort. *More like a snack.* The snap of a hungry jaw jarred Caleb, and he pushed back against the dark thought.

No eating Connie's pet. There were some lines even he wouldn't cross. Antagonizing his brother wasn't one of them. "Dude, whatever that funny looking hairball is, it's in the way."

"No, *she* is not. That's Princess's spot." Constantine reached in and stroked the tiny creature.

"Princess?" His level of incredulity rose a few more notches and teetered in the I-must-be hallucinating zone. *And yet I didn't snack on any mushrooms.*

"It's Princess Leia to be exact."

Bigger snort.

His brother shot him a look before turning back to his rat, crooning, "Ignore him, Princess. He doesn't understand your cuteness."

Cute? Had his brother been punched in the face one too many times? "Are you feeling all right?"

"Fine. Why?" His brother shot him a glance while still continuing to pet the hairy rat.

"I have to ask because I don't understand why a grown man would want to own something that wouldn't even double as a proper snack."

"Eat my dog and I will skin you and make you into boots." Judging by the hard flint in his brother's eyes, he meant it.

Caleb almost hugged him in thanks. Nice to see some things hadn't changed, such as their love of bodily-harm threats. Question was, would Constantine follow through?

Caleb should have let the matter go at that point. After all, loving a poor excuse for a dog wasn't the worse thing his brother could have done during Caleb's absence—*at least he didn't fuck up like I did*—but the fact that Caleb ranked lower than a pet stung. "It's a dog. Shouldn't it ride in the back?"

"No. And unless you'd rather walk, I'd suggest you get your ass on board. I've got better things to do than hang around here arguing with an a-hole."

Caleb's spine straightened, and he faced his brother, unable to hide the flatness in his eyes. "That wasn't very nice."

"Neither was what you did."

That stung, even if it was true. "I had my reasons."

"And I have mine. So choose."

Nice choice. Either tell his brother to fuck off and find his own ride, which would really set a tone. Beat the piss out of him and remind him that he was still the oldest? Or let his brother enjoy his petty revenge?

Doing the right thing really wasn't any fun.

I came back to make amends, not make things worse. So Caleb rode in the back while Princess got the passenger seat, perched pleased as punch in her basket that hung off straps wrapped around the headrest.

When Caleb asked what the heck that was, Constantine replied, "It's a booster for Princess so she can see out the window."

My brother's dog has a car seat. Meanwhile, Caleb didn't, but at least he had a ride, plus, on the bonus side, he and his brother had not yet come to blows, although it had been close.

I expect before the week is out, we'll exchange a few punches.

Constantine harbored a lot of anger and resentment. When Caleb had left home, his brother was just finishing high school, and given there were a few years between them, they hadn't really hung out much. It hadn't occurred to Caleb that the skinny runt—who'd packed on a good hundred pounds and a few inches since then—would resent his departure so much.

If sitting in the back of Constantine's truck was part of Caleb's punishment, then so be it. It wouldn't be the worst ride Caleb had ever gotten. At least this one didn't have gritty sand stinging at his eyes or snipers taking potshots.

As a matter of fact, he quite enjoyed the view and humid air until they hit the highway, whereupon Constantine made sure he hit the gas pedal hard. The truck shot forward with a burst of speed. No problem. Caleb leaned against the cab of the truck and crossed his arms. He could handle a little wind.

The rut in the road, however, almost sent him flying out of the bed of the pickup truck. He landed hard on his ass and couldn't help his irritation.

"Bloody hell, Constantine." Caleb banged on the window partition on the cab. "Take it fucking easy, would you?"

To which his little brother—who, at two hundred and eighty pounds of mean muscle, outweighed him—replied with an eloquent middle finger.

A laugh shook Caleb, a rusty sound that took him by surprise. It had been a while since he'd found something worth chuckling about. *It's good to be home.*

Coming home, to be specific, the prodigal son who'd strutted off to war, brash and full of himself, and now returned, a wounded veteran who—

"Is getting no goddamned respect!" he yelled as his brother plowed the truck through a puddle on the shoulder. On purpose. *Little bastard.*

He smiled.

The muddy water coating his skin and worn T-shirt couldn't diminish his contentment. Even out here, still practically in the city, the smells of the swamp surrounded him. Moist and thick, the humidity in the air revived him.

Since his departure from home, Caleb had spent years serving his country overseas in barren wastelands, where the gritty sand got in everything and the heat sucked the moisture from your skin, leaving it tougher than a croc's hide.

But he'd left the desert behind months ago. Spent some time up north in Alaska, a shifter-friendly town known as Kodiak Point, as a matter of fact. While hiding out there, he'd scrubbed and scrubbed at his skin until he could pretend the stink of smoke and burning flesh didn't cling to him. Some stains never came out, but they faded to the point where he now felt that he could face the world—scarred in both body

7

and soul. Time to complete his return to the real world and come home, a home that was the same and yet different.

A familiar pink billboard caught his eye. Look at that, Maisy's gift shop still did business on the edge of the highway. The next familiar ad was for Bayou's Bite, where a person could eat the best crab cakes in town. *They also used to make the best deep-fried shrimp and served the coldest beer.* He looked forward to seeing if that was still the case.

What he didn't enjoy seeing, as they headed toward his hometown, was the appearance of several subdivisions that had popped up along a few miles stretch of the highway. Ugh to progress. Not more cookie-cutter houses and townhomes.

Who the hell would want to live in one of those?

Not the folks from his town, that was for sure.

Welcome to Bitten Point, Florida. A tiny town hugging the Everglades and home to a shifter population that spanned a gamut of species, unlike the city groups that tended to cater to one breed and ran all others out.

Rumor had it, the wolves controlled New York and some other big cities out west while the lions owned Texas and Arizona. As for Montana and Colorado, that was bear country.

But down here, where the land was wet and the climate warm to scorching, shifters lived more or less in harmony. Except for that odd flock of Canadian Snow Geese. They spent half their years down south but kept to themselves.

But ignoring those birdbrains—which, rumor held, tasted best when basted with butter sauce—the rest of the shifters lived in peace. And if they didn't, then Big Jim, the mayor of their town, took them out to the swamp for a talking-to. Sometimes, he came back alone.

In the shifter world, justice was swift, and often without mercy. A secret like theirs couldn't be risked. Even though some humans knew of the existence of shifters, such as the higher levels in the military and government, the general populace remained ignorant.

And everyone worked to keep it that way.

A swerve of the truck had him gripping the sides as Constantine veered off the highway to take the main road into Bitten Point.

Getting closer…

His heart thumped a little bit faster, and his fingers tightened to the point that his knuckles turned white.

Don't panic now.

He'd done so well up to this point. Taking deep breaths, Caleb pushed the crippling anxiety back into its little box, a box that also contained a rather large reptile that wasn't too happy with Caleb right now.

Too fucking bad. His beast couldn't be counted on to behave, so it was best to keep him leashed.

For distraction, Caleb watched the side of the road. They should be coming across it soon… There it was.

The welcome sign to town loomed.

Bitten Point.

The image on the massive billboard consisted of a large gator head with its jaws wide open saying, "Welcome, won't you stay for a bite?" The colors had faded since he'd last seen it, and the population on it had moved from seven hundred and sixty-five to seven hundred and ninety-six.

Life had flourished while he was gone.

Just past the billboard, he couldn't help but note that the Itty Bitty Club had gotten a new sign, a neon monstrosity that showed the silhouette of a woman wearing a tiny bikini. An itty-bitty bikini.

For as much as the more puritan-minded tried to get it shut down, the strip club remained, offering visual entertainment, expensive beer, and jobs to those who didn't mind baring a bit of skin.

Main Street remained much the same with the town hall and post office sharing the same building. The grocery store had gotten a facelift, as a chain one had apparently moved in.

There was the pharmacy, right next door to the vet, whose practice had flourished evidently, given they'd also taken over the video emporium that used to fill the space alongside.

As soon as they left the main road, a rapid right turn that sent his ass skidding, signs of civilization, at least the modern kind, faded. Out here, this close to the Everglades, greenery took on a life of its own, determined to thwart progress's encroachment of its territory.

They were in bayou land now and, even better, shifter land.

In the movies and books, humans always feared the shifters living in the city, using the paved streets and alleys as their hunting ground. In reality, with the exception of a few groups, most shifters preferred to remain close to nature, to have quick and easy access to acres of wilderness so, when the beast needed to emerge, they didn't need to fear discovery—or bullets.

Even then, though, they had to be careful. Being a rather large crocodile in bayou country wasn't always a safe thing. Caleb didn't have the scars to prove it—only silver truly ever left a permanent mark, silver and fire to be specific—but he did remember the pain of getting shot.

Damn Wes and his not-so-funny pranks.

The truck turned suddenly, but having expected it, Caleb held on to the sides and let out a triumphant yell. "Missed!" A taunt that almost had him biting his tongue as his brother steered into a deep rut. "Bastard!" He yelled it with laughter, a humor that faded with each mile they got closer to his childhood home—and Ma.

There came that fluttery feeling again. But this was a normal trepidation, not the gut-wrenching fear when he heard the crackle of flame devouring tinder.

Would his mother be happy to see him?

Ma certainly hadn't been too pleased when he'd left, and they'd not talked since. His fault. He cut off everyone in his life. *Everyone...*

So how would Ma react to her son coming home?

He still remembered her parting words...

"That's it, leave, just like your father did. He didn't come back, and neither will you." She might have thrown the words at him with vehemence, but her voice had also choked with tears.

It was true his dad had joined the military, just like Caleb, except his dad hadn't come back alive.

The flag they presented his mother did not make up for the loss of the man who'd taught Caleb to fish and spit but who hadn't been around to teach him how to control the beast.

Not having a father as the reptile within matured, flooding Caleb with its cold views and voracious hungers, meant Caleb didn't have a mentor to teach him the tricks to remaining in control.

No one to teach him how to let the beast out safely.

Could he have asked for help from someone else? Yes. Did he? No.

Instead, I lost control.

Took a bite.

A bite that changed the course of his life. A fatal bite that forced him to leave the small town he'd grown up in, abandoning his family and deserting the one girl—

He punched himself in the leg, the hard blow veering his attention because he was not going there. For years he'd forced himself to not allow thoughts of *her.*

Don't start now. Renny is better off without me.

Chances were she'd gone on with her life. Settled down with someone. Someone who could treat her right and make her happy.

Who made that growling sound? Apparently it wasn't just the croc in his mind rising from his mental prison to snap its teeth that had a problem with Renny being with someone else.

Time hadn't diminished some things, such as his jealousy issues. He'd always had a she's-mine problem where Renny was concerned. Prettiest girl he'd ever seen and she'd chosen him.

But they couldn't tell anyone about it, not with her dad crazier than batshit, especially after a drinking binge, and his ma determined that he go to college and make something of himself instead of *"Settling down too young and missing out on life."*

At the time, all the reasons not to be together had made them only more determined.

Nothing better than sneaking out to her place and giving her a hand—on account he was such a gentleman—so she could climb out the window. The memory of those hours they spent under the starlight still had the power to arouse.

People often resorted to pills or toys or weird fantasies to bring excitement to sex, but Caleb still thought the hottest kind of fuck was the type where you were afraid of getting caught by someone's father. A man who kept a loaded shotgun by the door.

The tame sex he'd enjoyed later on, in a bed, just never could compare.

Or was it because no one could compare to Renny?

Don't go there. He gave himself a mental slap, and yet, no matter how many times he told himself to forget Renny, his thoughts always seemed to stray back.

The truck rolled to a stop, the crunch of gravel louder for a moment than the singing of the frogs and crickets.

Shit, I'm home.

For a moment, his breathing quickened, his pulse raced, and it wasn't the humidity that dampened his skin.

Don't panic. Breathe, dammit. Breathe.

Spots danced in front of his eyes, and he felt himself losing his grip. The croc swam to the surface, veering for the weakness and looking to escape.

No. I mustn't lose control.

Stupid anxiety attack. He'd hoped he was done with those. It had been weeks since his last good one.

This simmering bout proved all wasn't well yet in his mental landscape. But he could handle it. The doctor in Kodiak Point had taught him tricks to calm himself. And when all else failed, there were the heavy-duty pills.

But he couldn't just pop a few blue sleeping agents and drop off into a coma for a few hours. He needed to man up.

Step one. Take a deep breath.

Step two. Scratch his balls to remind himself he wasn't a prissy fucking princess.

Step three—

"What the hell are you doing?" Constantine said, snapping him back to the here and now.

Doing? Why having a panic attack, of course, but that wasn't something he was about to admit. "Just taking in all the changes to the place."

And there were plenty to provide distraction. For one, they now actually had a driveway of crushed stone rather than the mud and flattened weeds he recalled. The house that had once sported weathered, gray planks and mismatched shingles was still there, but massively face-lifted with white vinyl siding and a light blue metal roof.

"Are those fucking shutters?" Caleb asked in disbelief, taking in the new windows that had taken the place of the wooden-silled ones. How he'd hated those damned things. When it got truly humid they swelled so tight that they refused to open. When one did open, he'd smashed his fingers in them too many times to count because he didn't get the block of wood wedged under it in time.

"Not just any shutters, but hurricane-grade ones," Constantine replied, his upper body hidden within the truck. When his brother leaned back out, he had his little dog tucked under his arm.

"So that's what you did with my paychecks?" Just because Caleb had left home didn't mean he didn't try and improve his mother's lot in life and, by default, his brother's too.

"Not exactly. Mom used the checks to put me through college."

"Yeah, because you need a college degree to fish for shrimp and crabs," Caleb couldn't help but retort. Full-time college had never been a possibility for him when he finished high school. He'd gone straight to work to support his family and then struggled through the part-time classes at his local college until he quit them to be with Renny.

Constantine saw right through his cruel taunt. "I don't work in the bayou. Haven't since you left, really. Ma wanted to make sure I had a different set of choices when I graduated."

In other words, she didn't want a second son going off to war.

"The place looks good," he grudgingly managed to say.

"Thanks. Come on. We should go inside. Ma's probably got dinner ready for us. She's been cooking all day."

Just ignore the drool, as if he could help it at the thought of one of his ma's home-cooked meals. How long had it been since he'd enjoyed real food?

Stomach leading the way, Caleb vaulted from the truck bed and followed his brother toward the house.

Faced with a front door painted a dark blue, Caleb froze. This wasn't his home anymore. So much had changed. His home. His brother. *Me.*

Caleb wasn't the same guy who'd left years ago. And he never would be again.

I'm damaged goods. Both physically and mentally. He could handle the scars on the outside, even if within he cringed every time someone winced or grimaced at his appearance. What he still had a harder time with was the damned nightmares and panic attacks.

Was he so selfish that he would dump himself, and all his problems, on his brother and mother, who had obviously flourished in his absence?

"You know what. I think I should pop into town first. Maybe grab some groceries. Or flowers. Yeah. I need flowers." Caleb turned on his heel and had his hands on the raised edge for the bed of the truck to climb in when he found himself yanked backwards.

With a firm hand on each of Caleb's shoulders, Constantine frog-marched him to the front door. "Don't be such a pussy. Buy flowers?" Connie snorted. "Ma doesn't need anything but your ugly mug. Why, I don't know."

Neither did Caleb. They'd exchanged such ugly words. Angry ones. Hurtful ones.

Given he couldn't tell her the truth, they'd not spoken since. As a matter of fact, he'd not spoken to anyone in Bitten Point until he called a number he knew by heart and his brother answered.

With his eyes closed and spots dancing behind his lids, Caleb had asked, "Can I come home?"

To his surprise, Constantine said yes.

And now, here he was, shaking like the biggest fucking coward.

Before Constantine could force Caleb to climb the painted porch steps—with an honest-to-god railing—the door opened, and there was his ma.

Unlike the rest of home, she hadn't changed. Sure, there might be a few more gray hairs and a crease or two, but the blue eyes, the trembling smile, and the outstretched arms were—

Caleb took the steps in a single bound and yanked her into his grip.

In a voice choked—with a bug, dammit, never tears—he murmured, "I'm home."

Chapter Two

One more stop until I can go home.

Pulling into the driveway of the executive home, Renata Suarez—Renny to her friends—sat for a moment before getting out of her car. Every minute of every day it seemed as if she was rushing somewhere, having to do something. Sometimes she worried she'd get so damned busy she'd forget to breathe.

Heck, I'm lucky if I remember to feed myself sometimes. Good thing Luke was around to remind her that sustenance was required or she might have wasted away.

Yet, somehow, despite all the trials, she was making it. She was providing for her and her son, but at what cost?

I've barely seen him grow up. While the daycares she'd relied on over the years were great at taking pictures and videos, the sad fact was, Renny had missed Luke's first step, the first pee in a potty, and so many other milestones. *But what other choice do I have?*

The bills wouldn't pay themselves.

At least now that she'd returned home, she had Melanie caring for her son before and after school, and at a totally rock-bottom rate. Nothing.

As Melanie explained it, "I'm stuck at home anyways because of my hellions. Might as well have your angelic one here, too. You never know, maybe he'll rub off on my little demons."

How I love that girl. Melanie was the only reason why Renny hadn't left Bitten Point once her dad died. Her best friend was the only thing helping Renny keep her sanity right now, and given all Melanie had done to help, she shouldn't abuse her good will.

Stop lazing around, and go get your son. Exiting the car, she took a few strides to reach the door. Renny walked right into Melanie's house, just in time, too, judging by Melanie's shouted, "I'm going to make you both into rugs if you don't behave."

What were the boys doing now?

Stepping into the living room, Renny caught her best friend since kindergarten with her hands on her hips, hair wisping in curls around her face, and her dark brown gaze focused on two little boys perched on the backrest of the couch.

Those two imps eyed their mother, expressions rife with mischief. Without saying a word, Rory and Tatum leaped.

Melanie screeched, "Demon spawn!" and the boys laughed. The two mini acrobats bounced on the sofa cushions, not at all repentant.

It was hard not to smile, so Renny averted her head, lest the children see her amusement. She sought out her son, Luke, and found that he sat in the corner at the play table, head bent as he scribbled away. She stared at him for a moment, but he never looked up. He ignored her. It was so obvious by the tight set of his shoulders and the furious stroke of his crayon.

Her son was mad at her, and with good reason. She was late. Again.

I won't be winning the mother of the year award. But in

her defense, she worked two jobs, and neither of them would cut her slack. *"We're short staffed, which means you need to work later today."* Saying no wasn't an option when she needed that money to survive.

However, she did long for the day that she could tell Benny at the supermarket to take his job as a cashier and shove it in a very nasty spot. As for her nighttime waitressing, despite the late hours, that job she enjoyed, even if some nights her ass was slapped a few too many times for her liking. At least those nights meant good tips.

Renny snuck up behind her best friend, counting on the chortles from the twins to hide her approach.

Then she made Melanie jump. "Having fun again, are we? And yet you're thinking of popping the third?"

Visibly jarred, Melanie whirled. "Dammit, Renny, don't sneak up on me like that. I think I just wet myself."

The twins took that moment to listen to their mother, and their mouths made the roundest O of surprise, but not for long before they went into spasms of giggles, Rory chortling, "Mommy peed her pants." A pause then a yell from Tatum, "Again."

Melanie glared at her brood. "It's a good thing you're cute or else…"

Before anyone could think Melanie was a witch of a mother, it should be noted that she doted on those boys, and while she did mock-threaten them, she was the first to encourage them to explore the world. In other words, climb. Just not the furniture in the house. Her poor curtain rods couldn't handle any more abuse.

"Tickle monster attack!" Melanie yelled before diving at her boys. They scattered, high-pitched squeals along with the thump of bare feet on wood floors. Her friend wiped her arm across her forehead. "Whew. Those two are way too full of piss and vinegar today."

"A little wound up, were they?"

"More like unhinged," Melanie grumbled. "Must mean a storm is coming."

"When isn't a storm coming?"

"Good point. Given the silence, I've only got another minute or two before I need to hunt them down. The last time they disappeared for more than five minutes and were quiet, they slathered hand soap in the hallway and were using it as a slip and slide."

The antics of Rory and Tatum never failed to entertain. Luke didn't tend to such wildness, although, of late, his moods were more erratic. "How was Luke today?" Renny asked before kneeling by her son. He pointedly ignored her, the crayon dropped on the table so that he could thumb his Nintendo DS. He loved that toy, which made the scrimping she'd done to get it for him for Christmas worthwhile. But while he loved the game, it was now also a weapon he used to shut her out.

Ever since he'd begun school, her son had changed. Her shy and cuddly son now no longer wanted her to hold his hand in public, and he no longer crawled into her lap for stories.

He's only four. So young, and yet very much his own person. A little man without the guidance of a father, something he'd only begun to notice.

His immersion in the big wide world of the public school system meant he got to see how the

21

world worked. How other families lived. Not quite five years old, but perceptive for his age, he'd finally asked her not long ago the one question she never wanted to answer.

"Who's my daddy?"

"Why do you want to know?"

Luke had fixed her with a stare. "Other kids have a daddy. Who's mine?"

Did a no-good jerk who'd taken off and never looked back count? What about a guy who couldn't run away fast enough, breaking her heart while, at the same time, leaving her the biggest trial and treasure of all?

A son.

A son who had resorted to the silent treatment when she copped out and said, "I'll tell you when you're older." Weak. So weak.

Parenting fail, and yet telling him the truth now would not change anything.

For all intents and purpose, Luke's daddy was—

"Did you hear? Caleb's back in town."

Crouching didn't prevent the words from shaking her balance. Renny wobbled as she sucked in a sharp breath. Did something of her shock show in her features? Something must have because Luke finally deigned to look at her and asked, "What's wrong, Mommy?"

Wrong? Nothing. She didn't care what Caleb did. "Nothing is wrong..." She paused before saying baby. Last time she'd used the endearment, Luke was none too pleased. All part and parcel of him growing up. She could remember hating it when her dad called her drools. Only to wish he'd kept calling her that later in life. The time before her mother's death, before the drinking and the finding of God, were the years she tried to remember. Not what Daddy became after.

Renny realized her son was staring at her, having noticed she'd lost her train of thought. She quickly gathered herself. "I'm hungry, bug, are you? And since I won't have time to really cook supper for us tonight, what do you say we hit Bayou's Bite for a bucket of shrimp and fries before we go home?"

"You just wanna go home so you can leave me with Wanda." His lower lip jutted in a pout.

Way to slather on the guilt. *No need, baby. The guilt's always there.* She pinched her son's chin gently. "Sorry. I know I've been working a lot of hours lately. As soon as they hire some more people, I will have more time to spend with you." The promise she feared breaking only served to increase the guilt that gnawed at her, a nagging self-doubt that Melanie had been playing lately.

Her friend would never say anything in front of the kids, but Melanie's eyes clearly reminded Renny of the talk they'd had recently, given the bills were arriving bigger and faster than her paychecks. Broken muffler. Then a tire. The stove that died. Clothes and shoes for Luke. He was outgrowing things so quickly.

"You should go after him for child support," Melanie had said to her on the phone just last week. "He owes it to you."

"Caleb made it clear he wanted nothing to do with our baby." The jerk couldn't even be bothered to reply to her letters. She wasn't going to beg him or his family.

"You have to admit that doesn't sound like the Caleb we know."

Yeah, well, the Caleb she knew wouldn't have just decided one day to abandon family, home, and girlfriend to join the army with barely any notice, just a text message saying, *I enlisted. Don't wait for me.*

As breakups went, it had sucked.

And now Mr. Jerky-Pants was back, and she really didn't care. Now, could her foolish heart stop its ridiculous little flutter?

"What are you doing this weekend?" Renny asked as she watched Luke put on his shoes. God forbid she should offer to help. The little boy disdain was so clear, but her heart broke every time he said, "I can do this by myself."

"Doing?" Scrunching her nose, Melanie made a moue of distaste. "Andrew is making me go to some kind of corporate picnic they're having in the Glades behind the institute. As junior VP, he has to be there, which means, as his wife, I have to go. And wear a bra!" The travesty.

"Sounds like fun."

"Don't mock me. You know how I hate the swamp." Melanie's lips turned down. "The humidity kills my hair. An hour spent straightening it so it can turn into a giant fuzzball the moment I set foot in the bayou."

"I like your frizz."

This time, Renny earned the glare. "You shut your mouth, girl with the perfect, straight blonde hair. I swear, you could be outside in a hurricane and you still wouldn't need a brush. I hate you."

Wearing a smirk, Renny flipped her ponytail. "I hate you, too, and yet I'd still trade in a heartbeat. Although, I will warn you that the saying is false.

24

Blondes do not have more fun." She grimaced.

"Only because someone won't get someone to do something so she can have a life and do, you know, other someones." Melanie arched her brow as she referenced things obliquely.

Renny's mature reply was to stick her tongue out.

Having caught the final act, Luke sighed and, with a very put-out voice, said, "Mom. That is so immature."

She blinked at him then looked at Melanie. "Isn't he too young to use that tone with me? And that word? Who taught him a word like immature?"

"I blame YouTube," Melanie said. "It is the root of all evil and that rude fruit show." Renny went to step out, but Melanie leaned out after her and said, "Hey, so you didn't say what you were doing this weekend. If you're bored tomorrow, feel free to come to the picnic. I could use moral support."

"I thought those were called mint juleps."

"No drinking allowed." Melanie rubbed her belly.

"Are you…?"

"Not yet. But we're trying. I just went through my rounds of testing at the institute, and we'll be starting fertility treatments soon."

Opposite breeds in the shifter world had a harder time producing offspring than the same kind. With Melanie's inner animal being a panther, and her husband a bear—even if a poor excuse for one—they needed all the help they could get. However, because they had to keep their secret, just going to a regular doctor was out of the question. Lucky for Melanie, part of Bittech's purpose was to help shifters with medical conditions under the guise of pharmaceutical testing of the natural ingredients found in the bayou.

"Are you sure you're ready for a third one?" Renny asked softly. She knew things weren't exactly great between her best friend and her husband.

A moue twisted Melanie's lips. "I love being a mom. Although, I wish Andrew was more keen on being a dad. Don't get me wrong, though, he loves the boys." Said a touch more brightly than necessary.

Trying to convince Renny or herself?

Now wasn't the time to push. She'd wait until they could spend a few hours together killing a carton of cookie dough ice cream and listing all the faults with men. "Well, I hope you get pregnant, just so I can enjoy the desserts." A pregnant Melanie was a sweets craving and cooking one. As her best friend, Renny got to taste and take home many of the results.

"I'm going for a girl this time. A pair, if we're lucky, to make sure the numbers are even. Get off the kitchen counter. No more cookies!" she bellowed. Turning a sweet smile on Renny, Melanie, who possessed some kind of satanic blood to switch personas so quickly, asked, "So will you come tomorrow as my plus one?"

"I have a pile of laundry to do. And groceries. And…"

"And this is why your life is so boring. Stop being so damned responsible for once and do something fun."

"I'll think about it." Although Renny wasn't sure a company picnic was her type of fun. Besides, Melanie had an ulterior motive. An extra set of legs to hunt her precious imps down.

Speaking of whom...

Matching mischievous faces peeked and waved goodbye from between their mother's legs.

Renny blew them kisses, and they recoiled with harmonized, "Eews!"

To more shouted threats of "Don't you dare lock the bathroom door," Renny left with her son.

While Luke could open the car door and get into his booster himself, even buckle it, she still supervised. Surely this much autonomy for this age was wrong.

With her son safely strapped into his booster, she got behind the wheel of her older model car, something that came off the production line more than ten years ago. As she drove the road home by rote, she reflected. *Maybe I should take Luke to the picnic instead of the laundromat tomorrow.*

The free food at the picnic and the entertainment value might make up for the fact that she'd have to do the laundry one of her free nights the following week. At least for groceries, she could take Luke on Sunday. He liked it when she raced the cart down the aisles and then jerked to a halt before anyone caught them. Every time, he would fiendishly giggle as she emerged from the aisle looking prim and proper.

Or at least he used to. Her son didn't giggle so much anymore.

Not since she'd started working all those extra shifts and ignored the question in his eyes.

Hard to avoid him when you lived in a space that was only a few hundred square feet. Luke had the bedroom while she got to sleep on the couch. But it should be noted it was a damned comfortable couch.

Space wasn't the only issue. The apartment she and Luke called home wasn't exactly awash in amenities—a tiny electric stovetop, but no oven, a small fridge, and a single sink for dishes, but it was theirs, clean, and, best of all, affordable.

Because no way am I asking Caleb for money.

Her pride wouldn't let her beg that way.

However, looking over at Luke's short-cropped brown hair, she had to wonder. *Is my pride more important than my son?*

Chapter Three

The music thumped, strong enough to vibrate against the skin, a hard bass beat, and that was all that was really needed for the girl up on stage to strut her stuff. Leaning back in his seat, Caleb eyed the dancer's red leather boots. They looked new and still gleamed with that store-bought shine. Genuine pleather, unlike his snakeskin boots. Authentic skin, he might add. One of the few mementos Caleb had brought back from his time overseas.

The woman on stage wore a minimal amount of clothing. Actually, at this point in her routine, all she had left other than her boots was her thong. Less panty than a tiny scrap of fabric just enough to cover her shaven mound. As for her breasts, they shook and shimmied to the beat as she gyrated, still wearing a flirtatious smile.

For a moment, her gaze strayed to Caleb and then locked. He saw her eyes widen in recognition. She shot him a come-hither smile and a quick-winked invitation.

Cute, but not his type, and that was without even knowing who the hell she was.

As Caleb turned away to see what else was happening in the strip club, Daryl nudged him. "Would you believe that's Bobby's little sister?"

"Fuck off. That's Hilary? Damn. Last time I saw

her she was wearing braces and Bobby's old football jerseys."

"She grew up while you were gone. Hell, you should see my own sister. She's Miss Melly Homemaker now. She's even talking about popping kiddo number three."

"Damn, she's got kids?" Last time Caleb had seen Melanie, she was in her last year of high school. "Is your sister still with what's-his-name? That dude whose dad owns that big ass company in the area. Some kind of bio-medical research lab."

"Andrew? Yup. He's now a CEO with the company. Making good dough, too. My sister is living in that new swanky subdivision just outside of Bitten Point."

"Your sister is a yuppie housewife?" Caleb snickered. "Never thought I'd see that day." Not given how much of a tomboy Melanie had been growing up.

"Yeah, my mom is so proud. Apparently, owning a house with a dishwasher and more than one bathroom is an indication she's made it." Daryl rolled his eyes. "Apparently, having an in-house toilet and outhouse one just isn't the same."

Yet another smile stretched his lips. Daryl was a bayou man at heart. He'd never get caught dead in a suit or living a cookie-cutter life.

"I see you've managed to evade getting hitched. Whatever happened to Stacy what's-her-name that you were dating?"

A shudder shook his friend. "Stacy was over like a month after you left. She started talking marriage and babies, and I started talking leaving civilization behind and living off the land..." Daryl shrugged as he grinned. "As it turns out, she wasn't wanting the same things in life I was."

Caleb chuckled and shook his head. Nice to see his best friend hadn't changed. He had to admit he'd wondered what Daryl would do when he showed up at his mom's front door right after dinner—a dinner consisting of a droolingly delicious homemade clam chowder with Ma's special cornbread for dipping.

Caleb had no sooner tucked away two platefuls than someone rang the doorbell.

"Since when do we have a fucking doorbell?" Caleb exclaimed.

"Language," his ma chided in the midst of clearing the table.

"We have a doorbell because I spent thirty bucks to get one. Just because we live by the swamp doesn't mean we can't have amenities," Constantine informed him.

A doorbell, shutters, and new laminate flooring in every room. What had happened to the charming shack he'd grown up in? Caleb could no longer see the marks of his past—they'd painted over some of his best penwork!

As Princess took off for the front door, barking and bristling like a rabid squirrel, Caleb followed after, not out of any interest in who was at the door, but more a wonder if the tiny dog would rip whoever dared come to the house into shreds.

She was certainly freaking out enough to make Caleb think she was perhaps part hound of Hell.

Opening the door, he had no trouble recognizing who stood there. Daryl.

Awkward.

Ma and Constantine weren't the only ones Caleb had more or less abandoned without a word. How had his best friend taken his abrupt departure?

Daryl took a hard look at him and said, "You know you're a dickhead, right?"

"Biggest dick around," Caleb retorted.

To which Daryl smirked. "Not according to the ladies." And that was that. His Latino friend sauntered in and hugged his mother.

Now some people might wonder at Melanie and Daryl's very non Hispanic names. Simple. Their mother was convinced that in order to succeed in the world, they needed a proper name. A very English name. Although, as Daryl once confided to Caleb, the name wasn't what slammed doors in his face, but his tanned skin, tattoos, and attitude. Raised on the wrong side of the bayou, it didn't matter what they wore or how they spoke, people judged. But guess what? Caleb didn't give a fuck and neither did his best friend.

Apparently, Daryl had not been a stranger to his home in Caleb's absence. Perhaps that was why his mother told him—after a dessert of homemade peach-flavored ice cream—that they should go out and enjoy themselves.

Whatever the reason for her wanting to get rid of him, Caleb took it, not eager to get into a conversation with his ma that would prod him about things he'd prefer to bury. See, the thing was, despite the need for secrecy, he wasn't sure he could lie to his mother anymore.

But what about Daryl? He'd probably have questions, too, so Caleb warned him. "I don't know if I'm ready to talk about the last few years."

"I'm not a fucking idiot. It's obvious something serious went down. Why else would you have fucked off in the middle of the night without a word hardly to anyone?"

"I had my reasons."

"I'm sure you did, and I'm sure they're valid, but it doesn't mean it wasn't still a dick move. Lucky for you, though, I've been a dick a time or two in my life, so I know it can happen. However, I do insist you buy me a beer. To remind me why you're my friend."

Just knowing Daryl still considered them friends had Caleb buying a pitcher and telling the waitress to keep them coming. And they weren't cheap pitchers, seeing as how they were ordering them in a strip club.

The Itty Bitty Club—featuring the ittiest thongs and most fabulous titties around—resembled every other exotic dancing bar with tables with enough space between them to give a man a bit of room—so the dancers would come by and offer a little more personal time. The place was cleaner than most. The scarred wood surfaces might have seen a cloth before he sat down. No sticky spots or moisture rings to be seen.

Just don't touch under the table.

The chairs all had armrests, for the entertaining ladies' benefit. It gave them something to hold on to as they lap danced for a large bill or two. Panties on and no body parts grinding didn't mean a gal couldn't straddle the chair and air hump.

Not Caleb's thing, in public at least.

Having gone to strips joints more than a couple of times, Caleb knew the best spot was by the bar, chatting up the usually pretty bartender while watching the show on stage in the mirror.

His buddy, however, had other plans.

"Let's get up close," Daryl had said, leading the way to the stage.

"Why? Seen one, seen them all."

Daryl kept walking and found a vacant spot.

Caleb followed and dropped into the open chair across from his bud.

This is as close as you can get.

Sitting in pervert's row meant Caleb had a great glimpse of the action on stage. Daryl quite enjoyed the show, calling out to the girls, apparently knowing most by name. After a while, Caleb realized he knew quite a few of those gals, too.

"Is that so-and-so?" followed by a "yup" formed the bulk of several conversations. Relaxing. No pressure. Some of his tension eased.

I'm safe here.

Or so he thought until Daryl broke the pattern with a muttered, "Shit. She wasn't supposed to be working tonight."

"Who are you talking about?" Caleb no sooner said the words than awareness made him stiffen. A tingle swept across his senses, a familiar, longed-for touch.

Uh-oh. It couldn't be her. No way. No way could he still feel her in that intimate way he used to so many years ago.

I must be wrong. I mean think, idiot, she would never work in a place like this. Renny was always so damned classy. And let's not forget her daddy would never let her.

Wrong.

What he thought he knew had changed, but Renny hadn't.

34

Holy fuck, she's more beautiful than I remembered.

Long blonde hair swept into a ponytail showing off the long column of her neck. A figure a little more round than before, but utterly sexy. As to her face... A few years of maturing had taken her soft girlish features and sculpted them. *She's a woman now.*

A ridiculously attractive one, and for the first time since they'd entered the strip club, Caleb had to drop his hands into his lap—so he could mash his fist against his daring-to-stir cock.

Stay down.

Seriously. Getting an erection for her was probably perverse. Titties bouncing all over the place, practically in his face, did nothing, but seeing the one woman in the world who probably hated him, and was clothed to boot, turned him on?

At this point, he should note that while Renny did wear clothes, they were exceedingly sexy and skimpy. In his view, they were not appropriate for this bar—or public viewing.

What does she think she's doing strutting around in that tight-fitting crop top? A shirt that molded to her perfect handful of tits. And who thought those itty-bitty jean shorts she wore, that barely covered her full ass, were appropriate work attire?

Doesn't she know how sexy she fucking looks? What a temptation she poses?

Why the hell did he care so much? Agitated, he turned his attention back to the reason he was feeling the tension creeping back in. Daryl had done this.

Caleb growled. "What the fuck is she doing here?"

Hands raised, Daryl shook his head. "Sorry,

dude. I honestly didn't know she'd be here. She doesn't usually work here Fridays."

Usually? "Are you saying she works here on a regular basis?"

"Has been since not long after the baby."

He choked on his sip of beer. "Baby?"

"Dude, did you not keep up on any of the news in town?"

"No." Because a part of him didn't want to know.

"Lots of stuff has been happening."

So he kept being reminded. "Who's she hooking up with?" Because he totally wanted to plant his fist in his face. *Rip into him and kill him.*

He ignored the suggestion. He most certainly suffered from a green problem, but it wasn't jealousy.

Daryl shrugged. "No one that I know of lately."

"What about the baby's daddy? Is he still in the picture?"

"Nope. Not that anyone knows who it is. She went off not long after you left to care for an aunt or something. She came back about six months ago with a kiddo."

"And no one knows who the father is?

Daryl shook his head. "She won't say. All my sister will say is that he was a jerk who wasn't ready for the responsibility."

A certain right fist wanted to show an asshole what happened when he ditched his responsibilities. Caleb knew what it was like to grow up fatherless. Despite the fact that Renny probably hated him for leaving, Caleb didn't like knowing she was struggling.

But that still didn't excuse her choice of work.

Caleb stood abruptly, the chair screeching back against the floor. "I need to see her."

Reaching out, Daryl grabbed his arm as he went to walk by. "Dude, don't do it."

"Do what? Say hello to an old friend?"

"You guys were more than friends. Everyone thought you were going to get hitched. And then you left. No warning. Nothing. She was hurting. Bad. You can't blame her for mistakes she might have made."

Mistake? He'd left, and she had a baby by another man.

He should have been happy to know she'd moved on. Instead, he wanted to kill something.

Biting is good.

He ignored the voice. He did that a lot, and he didn't give a shit what that damned shrink said. Some things were better left locked away.

Because some acts couldn't be unseen.

"I don't know why you think I'm going to blame her for anything. I just want to talk to her. Say hi. Let her know I'm back." And that there were many nights he wished he'd never left.

Seeing her again reminded him of the most precious thing he'd lost.

Yet not leaving was never a choice.

Talking to her would prove a cruel form of torture, but he couldn't stop himself, even as Daryl reminded him, "Dude, don't do it. She knows you're back. Trust me, she knows. So sit down and have another beer. Or, even better, let's take off and go to the Bitten Saloon. It's a short stagger to my place then."

"You know I hate Western. And you're

worrying for nothing. Better I get this out of the way now. We were bound to run into each other at one point." Caleb had just hoped he'd find himself better armed when he did—like with a gun so he could shoot any asshole who dared to touch his girl.

Or we could eat them.

The cold thought wasn't his own. He paid it no mind, just like he paid Daryl no mind. Gaze narrowed, he made his way across the room. People wisely stepped out of his way. Could it be the intense glower he wore as he watched a certain pert ass—*an ass I groped too many times to count*— sashayed away? He followed.

Renny ducked into the women's washroom. Did she think to escape him? Caleb was a master when it came to getting his prey. It was what had gotten him into this situation.

I'm coming to get you. Given the women's public washroom was in a strip joint, and the employees had their own behind the scenes, Caleb felt pretty safe following.

No screams as he entered, a good sign, but neither did Renny acknowledge his presence. She knew he was there. She could see him approach in the mirror, just like he could see the tight set of her shoulders and the thin press of her lips.

A peeved-looking woman who sounded it, too. "You made a wrong turn. This is the women's washroom."

Ignoring her welcome, he said, "Hello, baby." The familiar nickname purred from him, unbidden, but once spoken, unable to be retrieved.

A long time ago, that endearment might have once curled her lips into the most beautiful smile. Now it just served to make her eyes flash with anger. "Don't you baby me, Caleb. I have no interest in talking to you."

"I get that, and I don't blame you."

"How magnanimous of you," she retorted dryly.

"You look good." Again, he spoke without thinking—or filtering. *I'd better start watching my words, or I'm going to get myself in trouble.*

Too late. He was in trouble the moment he came seeking her.

At his praise, she sucked in a breath, and a slight flush heightened the color in her cheeks. "You look good, too," she said.

At her obvious lie, his lips tightened. "I'm very much aware of how I look. No need to coddle me." The burns had left a scar, not just on his skin but his psyche. Even if she could ignore the one, he couldn't ignore the other.

"Coddle? I can assure you that would be last thing I'd do for you."

Renny always did have that irritating tendency of telling the truth, but even if she didn't find his scars ugly, that changed nothing.

"As you can see, I'm back."

"So everyone keeps telling me," she mumbled. "As if I care. I stopped caring a long time ago."

A lie that hit him hard and low. *She still feels something for me.*

Yeah, lots of anger.

"I know you hate me, and I just wanted to tell you that I'm going to do my best to stay away from you." Even if all he wanted was to stick to her like honey on a bear.

39

Her brow arched. "So far you're not doing a good job staying away."

"I thought I should talk to you because I figure we'd bump into each other again at some point, and I didn't want it to be awkward."

"Oh, because this isn't awkward at all." Renny rolled her eyes. "You've said hello. I know you're back. I also don't care, so if you don't mind, there's the door. Use it." She turned her back to him.

Oddly enough, though, he didn't want to leave. As a matter of fact, all he really wanted to do was snare her in his arms and squeeze her tight. Tell her how much he'd missed her and wished things could have been different. He wanted to peel that tiny shirt from her and cover her body in his. Surround her in his scent. Claim her and make her off-limits to others.

The time apart hadn't cooled the attraction on his part at all, but he wouldn't act on it.

Mustn't mark her and claim her and keep. She deserves better.

Thing was, he needed to make sure she hated him because, if she softened at all, like she did now with her body trembling slightly, he might not be able to resist. "So do you strip for money on top of waitressing? Or do you just strut your shit for every dick with a few dollars?"

She whirled on him. "Are you seriously insulting me here?"

"Just questioning your choice in careers." Because he knew she was capable of being more than a waitress in a strip club. "Couldn't you find something a little more—"

"More what? Morally sound? More clothed?

Perhaps you'd like me to walk two feet behind men and curtsy when they speak to me?"

"Now you're exaggerating. I'm just saying a nice girl like you should have higher aspirations than working in a titty bar."

"There is nothing wrong with working here. And that's a priceless thing to say, given you came here in the first place. If this place is so disgusting, then what are you doing here?"

Getting a beer? But he didn't have time to voice his reason. Renny was still talking, her voice reaching an incredulous pitch.

"You've got a lot of nerve, Caleb Bourdeaux, coming back into town after everything that's happened and acting as if I owe you anything or give a fiddle what you think."

Once again, he just couldn't seem to keep his mouth shut. "Maybe you should give a damn what I think since no one else seems to be. You deserve a job that doesn't require you dressing like this. For fuck's sake, Renny, your shirt is so tight I can see your damned bra."

"Are my bralines bothering you? Let me fix that."

He could only gape in shock as her hands slid under the fabric of her top, and in moments, she'd managed to unsnap her bra and slide her arms through the straps. She tossed the scrap of fabric at him.

It hit him in the chest, but he clasped it before it could fall. The cottony material still held the warmth of her body. Was it him or the beast that lifted it for a sniff?

Vanilla. Delicious. And tempting, just like the

buds of her nipples clinging to the material of her shirt that drew his gaze.

I am in so much trouble.

A trouble he couldn't seem to stop from snowballing.

"What are you doing with my bra?" she asked as he stuffed it in his pocket.

"Keeping it."

"For what?"

Nothing could have stopped his slow, lazy smile. "Inspiration."

It took her only a moment to grasp his meaning, and then she blushed. "Give it back right now. I will not have you—um. You know." Renny stumbled instead of saying the words.

"You gave it to me. It's rude to ask for a present back," Caleb chided.

But Renny didn't seem to care about bad manners. "I hate you." She stomped past him, the skin of her arm lightly brushing him, enough for an electric sizzle. Perhaps she felt it, too, because she stopped and whirled. Her brown eyes sparked. Her lips parted. "Actually, you know what, I do owe you something."

She leaned toward him, and he found himself angling toward her, too, already forgetting his promise to stay away. To—

"Ooomph!" Breath burst from him as she slugged him in the gut.

"That was for being an asshat and leaving." She kicked him in the shin. "That's for ignoring me after. And this is because I hate you!" She kneed him in the groin.

It did not feel good at all, but that wasn't the

reason he was breathless and in pain. His agony came not from her blows, but because she'd unleashed the full fury of her devastation.

A wave of emotions assailed him, crushing him with their rawness.

He dropped to his knees, burdened by the weight.

Is this how she truly feels?

So betrayed. Forgotten. Unloved. So lonely…

Still breathless, he couldn't say a word, only reach out to her, but she stepped back from his hand.

"Stay away from me, Caleb. Please." Keeping her gaze away from his, but unable to hide the tears glistening in her eyes or mask the roughness of her voice, she whirled once again and stomped away. She slammed through the swinging door.

And the world lost all hint of life and color.

For a moment, Caleb kneeled, staring at the door that had swung shut. Talk about blown away, and stunned, not just by her revelation of her feelings but her actions.

She hit me.

Sweet, gentle Renny had hit him. She'd even raised her voice and used the A word. *She called me an asshat.* Renny never cussed. He should know. Once upon a time he'd made her speak aloud the dirtiest words. How he loved the way she blushed and stammered saying just the word "damn."

But she wasn't just using stronger language, she hadn't been afraid to get physical and confrontational.

A forceful Renny. He didn't know what to think of it. She'd changed an awful lot. Because of him? Or was it because of this baby she had, the one she was raising on her own?

For some reason, knowing she had no one to help bothered him, and it wasn't just because he'd grown up without a dad.

Something of his trouble must have shown as he slid back into his seat across from Daryl.

"Nice mug. By the look of you, I take it things didn't go well."

"No. They didn't." And, yes, he might have said it rather sulkily. Despite all his protestations that he should stay away from Renny and she was better off without him, apparently a tiny part of him, that had remained hidden until this very moment, had hoped for a different outcome. Optimism fantasized she would fling herself into his arms and sob how much she'd missed him and still loved him.

I hoped that she loved me still.

However, it wasn't just their showdown in the bathroom that shattered that dream, but the fact that she'd birthed a child. A child she created with another man.

It bothered him. Someone else had touched her. Yet what had he expected?

I expected her to wait for me.

Yet, while he might have harbored that foolish fantasy, he'd certainly not abstained from the opposite sex. *I might have sated some needs, but I never loved them.*

Not like he'd love a certain golden-haired girl.

A girl who'd grown into a woman.

A woman determined to ignore him.

If only he could do the same, but he wasn't having the same kind of luck. In his defense, he wasn't the only one checking out the hot chick serving drinks in short shorts, getting her ass slapped and taking it with a smile while he seethed.

"Dude, that is a serious brood you've got going," Daryl said, waving his hand before Caleb's face and breaking his stare.

"I don't brood."

"Fine, glower. Scowl. Whatever. You need to stop. Renny's not interested, dude, so give it a rest."

But Caleb didn't want to give it a rest, which was why, when Daryl insisted on driving him home, he got out a few miles from home and claimed he needed to walk the rest of the way to clear his head.

Caleb wasn't lying completely. He did walk. Just not home.

Chapter Four

Still shaken after her encounter with Caleb, after the club closed just after one, Renata took her time wiping down the tables and gathering her things.

Being warned Caleb was in town and seeing him in the flesh were two totally different things. For one, she'd not expected the sharp pang of longing when she saw him again.

How can I still want him?

He'd changed so much. Definitely not the same carefree guy she'd known years ago. Yet, for all the cynical hardness in his features, the sneer on his lips, all those signs he bore that showed he'd faced danger and hardships, drew her even more.

It didn't hurt that he had a rocking body.

A fit guy when they dated, he'd passed in shape into superbly toned. His snug T-shirt had hugged his upper body, revealing broad shoulders, a defined set of pecs, a flat stomach, and arms that could squeeze the life from her.

She almost wished he'd try. How long had it been since she'd enjoyed a hug from a male other than her son?

But Caleb was the wrong person to be craving a hug from.

I hate him, remember?

Right. Hated.

Yet craved.

Abhorred.

Yet her senses tingled.

Wanted to kill.

Yet he made her feel alive.

Even now, with him gone for hours, awareness tickled all of her nerves, a hyper-sensitivity that initially let her know where he was at all times when he was in the club. She might not have an inner beast like most folks in town, but that never stopped her from knowing when Caleb was nearby. Melanie used to call it fate.

Now Renny had to wonder if it was a warning?

Whatever the cause, it made it so hard to ignore him. It didn't help that he kept watch on her while she worked. If she happened to turn and peek, there he was, staring at her, hunger lighting his gaze, stark longing drawing lines in his face.

It might have made a weaker woman melt. Not her. He wasn't going to win her back with either his looks or his attention.

Too bad. So sad. This ship has sailed. You had me once and look at what happened.

Caleb had dumped her ass and gone to war. So what if he returned? So what if he'd obviously suffered judging by the scars he bore? Being only human, she wondered what happened to his face. The scar with its distinctive flat shine spoke of a terrible burn, one that went down his cheek, spotted his neck, and disappeared into the collar of his shirt. How far did it extend?

I wonder if he'd let me find out.

For curiosity's sake, of course, not sensual.

Did it still hurt? She had to wonder if it was why he acted so jaded. So prickly.

Is he trying to keep people away from him?

That wasn't the Caleb she knew, who thrived on hugs and snuggles.

Given the direction of her thoughts, she wasn't too surprised when she exited the building to see Caleb leaning against her car.

She halted in the doorway, torn with indecision. *Am I ready to deal with him?* Would she ever be? Caleb was right in one respect. In a town this size, they couldn't avoid each other forever.

Bruno grumbled from his spot by the door, the red tip of his cigarette glowing bright. "Bloody stalkers. Stay put here for a second, Renny, would you? It will only take me a second to chase that bottom feeder away."

Placing a hand on Bruno's arm, Renny stopped him. "It's okay. I know the guy. He won't hurt me." Because he no longer had the power to hurt her. He'd already done his worst.

"Are you sure? I don't mind crunching him up." As a big bull gator, Bruno meant that quite literally.

Living in the bayou meant accepting certain rules. The first one being shifters made their own rules and they were quite often violent.

"If I need you to smash his face in, I'll let you know. Thanks, Bruno."

"Bah." He scoffed. "I'd do it for fun. Anyhow, I'm going to be here for another half hour locking things down. You need me, just holler."

"I will." Renny stepped away from the safety of the hulking bouncer and strode to her car. She tried to appear nonchalant, but inside, her heart raced. What did Caleb want?

When she was close enough not to shout, she asked, "Why are you stalking my car? I thought we'd said all there was to say inside." And she'd also imagined a whole hell of a lot after she realized what Caleb meant to do with her bra. Every time her hand wrapped around a tall glass, she couldn't help but be reminded.

"I didn't like the thought of you being out here all alone at night. Who knows what kind of creeps are lurking?"

"Calling yourself a creep now? That's harsher than what I would have said. More like clingy and unable to let things go." She stopped a few steps from him, head cocked at an angle as she stared at Caleb, trying to read the mysterious workings of his mind. She came up blank.

"I am not clingy."

"Oh, that's right, you're not, or you wouldn't have dumped me."

His lips thinned. "I had my reasons."

"I hope they were damned good ones." Should she mention there wasn't a reason valid enough to justify his actions?

"They were."

"Good enough to justify leaving me and, other than a measly text, never contacting me again?"

"I said I had my—"

"Reasons? Yeah. Whatever. Move away from my car. I need to get home."

"I'm coming with you."

She gaped at him before gathering her wits. "Oh

no you aren't. I can drive myself."

Caleb snorted. "I should hope you can drive, seeing as how I've had too many beers."

"You must have if you thought bugging me for a ride after work was a smart idea."

"Actually, I had a ride with Daryl, but I came back."

Curiosity made her ask. "Why?"

"Like I said, to keep an eye on you and make sure no one bothered you."

"People bothering me isn't your business. I'm not your business. And I don't need you waltzing into my work, giving me hell, and then stalking me after just because we used to date."

Caleb leaned toward her. "Come on, baby, you know we did more than date. We made love in every which way possible."

"I was young and gullible."

"We were horny for each other."

Yes, they were. Sometimes, at night when she was alone, she could still feel the heat and sensual thrill of his hands on her skin, the exhilarating rush of climax.

His reminder made her flush, even as she sputtered, "You're gross."

"No, I'm honest."

A bitter laugh erupted as she latched onto the word. "Honest? Really? That's priceless coming from you. Honesty from the man who ditched me with a text message and even now won't tell me why. Was it something I did?"

He didn't even hesitate. "Of course not."

"Were you in love with someone else?"

"Never!" The word burst from him with force.

"Then tell me why you left."

"I can't."

She exploded. "You are unbelievable. And not just with me. Everyone. Your family. Your friends."

He clamped his lips.

"Why won't you even try and defend yourself?"

"It wouldn't matter if I did. You wouldn't believe it, and I won't use it as an excuse. I treated you bad. I treated a lot of people bad, and I guess now I need to see if I can make amends."

The pieces clicked into place. "Oh, I get it now, this whole stalk Renny thing is about you trying to assuage yourself of your guilt. Dumped Renny, let's apologize and make it all better. Because it's so simple." As if words could heal what he'd done. But, if he thought she forgave him, would he leave her alone? "You know what, on second thought, I accept your apology. I forgive you for running off like a coward. You can cross me off your to-do list." *And get out of my life.*

"An apology isn't enough. I want to help you. You shouldn't be working at the Itty Bitty. You're better than that."

She arched a brow. "Too good for a paycheck? I gotta pay my bills like everyone else, Caleb. Some of us have responsibilities."

A frown drew his brows together. "So I hear. But you shouldn't shoulder the burden alone. Maybe you should force a certain asshole father to give you some help so you don't have to degrade yourself working in a place like this." Caleb swept his hand at the bar behind him.

51

"My dad died, and even if he hadn't, he wouldn't have raised a finger to help me, not after the baby." A Bible-thumping fellow, Dad had stopped talking to her, and even on his deathbed from a vicious fever he'd caught in the bayou, he turned his head away when she went to say her goodbyes.

"I wasn't talking about your dad. I was talking about your baby's father. It takes two to make a kid."

Her gaze narrowed. Hold on a second… "What about Luke's father?"

"Way I hear it, the deadbeat skipped out on you and the child."

"He did." Was he pulling her leg?

"That's not right," Caleb growled.

"No. It isn't." Incredulity built in her. Surely she was wrong.

"You should force him to take responsibility for his actions."

"You really think so?"

He nodded. "Make the asshole pay."

Sweet baby corn, he really didn't know. "Well, I'm glad you think so, Caleb, because given you ignored the letters I sent you, I kind of figured you had washed your hands of us."

He went still and turned pale. "What are you talking about? What was in those letters?"

"First, let me ask you, did you get them?" Judging by the panicked look in his eyes, he had. "Did you even open them?" He didn't have to answer for her to guess. A bitter laugh erupted. "Nope. You didn't bother, did you? Just chucked them in the trash, just like you did me and your son."

Nope, he didn't know, and she wondered if he'd

remember seeing as how he hit the ground pretty hard. She didn't stick around to find out.

Chapter Five

Your son.

The words echoed long after the last rumble of her car died off. Caleb lay on the ground as if frozen. And perhaps he was. He certainly didn't feel anything through the numb shield of his shock.

We have a child together.

No, not together. Renny had the child alone. All alone without anyone to rely on. Without telling a soul, not even his brother or mother because she thought he didn't want it.

Thought he didn't want her.

"Awwwww!" His yell echoed in the sky, and yet it did nothing to ease the bursting tension in him. His beast throbbed below the surface. Drawn by the rage. Fighting for control.

No.

No!

He had to keep his inner self caged.

But I have a son!

A son he was kept from by secrets and deals and a past he couldn't escape.

Except hadn't he escaped?

Caleb had retired from the military unit that had used him. He had escaped his servitude under the crooked rhino sergeant who drew him and others into acts of evil. A certain viperous enemy no longer controlled him.

Caleb couldn't help but touch the scar on his cheek. The price of slipping the naga's mesmerizing leash. Escaping the life he'd never wanted had left its mark, but he welcomed it. That scar signified his freedom, but it also reminded him of how it got there.

As if his nightmares would ever let him forget.

A shadow blocked the wan quarter moon struggling to shine in the sky. A blocky figure stood over him. Red slitted eyes flashed. A gator. Big one, too. *Wonder if he's another one of Wes's cousins?* The Mercers bred like bunnies on fertility drugs, popping kids out all over the place.

"There's no parking or sleeping in the lot overnight," the behemoth said.

"I seem to have lost my ride."

Luckily for him, Bruno wasn't a bad sort—even if he was a damned Mercer. He let Caleb borrow his phone, and that was why, less than twenty minutes later, his brother, glowering behind the wheel of his truck, pulled into the empty lot of the club.

Lowering his window, Constantine snapped, "Get in."

To Caleb's surprise, his brother leaned over and opened the passenger door.

"Holy shit, I get to ride in the truck."

His brother didn't crack a smile. "Only because Princess is sleeping in my jacket."

"Thank God because I was wondering what that bulge was in your lap."

His brother didn't say a word as he drove, but Caleb, for some reason, felt a need to spill. "So it turns out I've got a kid."

The truck swerved. "What?"

"His name is Luke. He's mine and Renny's."

The sudden forward momentum meant Caleb braced himself on the dash as the truck slammed to a stop.

"Get out of the truck," his brother ordered.

"Why would I do that?" Caleb asked.

"Why? Do you seriously have to ask? You know, I can handle the fact that you ditched me and Ma. I get it. I was almost eighteen. It wasn't like I needed you around. But to leave Renny and your kid?" Constantine banged his hands off his steering wheel. "I don't fucking know who you are. But you are not my brother. The brother I knew would never have abandoned his kid." Constantine shoved at him, and it was only the fact that the door was shut that Caleb didn't end up sprawled on the gravelly shoulder. As it was, Con's blow to his arm rocked the truck.

"Before you fucking hang me out to dry, I didn't know."

His brother's gaze narrowed. "What do you mean you didn't know? Didn't she tell you?"

Looking his brother in the eye as he admitted his fault proved impossible. "She tried to let me know. She sent letters. I just never read them."

"Just like you never read our letters, wrote back, or called us. You are such a fucking dick. Get out."

Couldn't argue that point. When Caleb would have opened the door, his brother growled, "Close the goddamned door." Constantine threw the truck into gear and, with a spin of the tires on the loose rock, drove them back onto the road. They drove for about a mile in silence before his brother said, "So I'm an uncle. To Luke."

"You've met him?" Caleb asked, suddenly thirsty to know more about his son.

"More like seen him. Once you left, Renny did for a while, too. I guess so that people wouldn't know she was pregnant."

"Kind of hard to hide, given she came back with a kid."

"Except she didn't come back right away. She's only been back in town about six months or so. I guess she felt like she had to on account of her dad. He caught some kind of disease or something, and she returned to care for him."

"Renny never told anyone he was mine?"

"No."

He couldn't help a pang at the knowledge she didn't want people to know Luke was his son.

But I can't really blame her, given she thought I didn't want him.

His brother slammed the wheel of his truck. "Dammit, I can't believe Renny never told me or Ma the baby was yours. We would have helped her if we'd known."

"As would I." Caleb slumped in his seat. "I've so royally fucked up my life."

"Yeah, you have."

"Gee, thanks."

"You didn't coddle me growing up, and I am not going to coddle you. You made mistakes. Suck it up, buttercup."

"You do realize I am supposed to be the older brother?"

"Then act like one. Or at least stop with this

fucking woe-is-me routine. Now that the truth is out, you can be a father to a little boy."

A father…

A wave of vertigo gripped Caleb, and he grasped the console of the truck, lest he face plant into it. "Shit, Con, I can't be a dad. I don't know how. Look at me. I'm a bloody mess."

"You're just like every other soldier who's come home after seeing and experiencing bad stuff. You need time to adjust. You're going to have to learn to adapt. And you need to stop feeling sorry for yourself and accept that shit has happened. Move on, bro. Start anew."

"But I don't know how." Even admitting the weakness made him want to cringe. His croc certainly thrashed in its hidden box, rolling and rolling, ashamed that he feared the fight.

"None of us do, which is why we wing it and we make mistakes. That's life, and she's a bitch." An assertion punctuated by a tiny growl within Constantine's coat.

"Easy to say, but what should I do?" For the first time in years, Caleb didn't have clear orders. He had to make the decisions. What if he made the wrong ones?

"First off, ask yourself what you want to achieve."

"What do you mean?"

Constantine took his gaze off the road for a minute to fix him with a stare. "What do you want to happen here? Set yourself a goal."

"You mean I should establish a mission objective."

"Wow, the military really did brainwash you. Okay, grunt"—Con flashed him a smile— "here's your mission. Assimilate into life at Bitten Point. Within that scope, you are to become involved with your son."

"If Renny lets me." Which was doubtful at the moment.

"Which brings me to the grovel-to-Renny-in-apology aspect. Add in to that make amends to Mother."

"And irritate my little brother." Caleb couldn't help but toss that one in and then laughed at the mock punch thrown by Constantine.

With Con's help in coming up with a clear mission, it occurred to Caleb that he needed allies, and that was why he found himself on Melanie's porch—in cookie-cutter suburbia where his borrowed pickup truck covered in mud looked like it belonged to a gardener not a visitor.

But at least he looked somewhat respectable. He'd managed a comatose night of sleep with the help of pills and had enjoyed a hearty breakfast cooked by his mother before she went off to work.

When Constantine had a buddy from work grab him on his way, leaving Caleb with some wheels, he had no excuse. Time to work on completing the first part of his mission.

Taking a deep breath, telling the nervous butterflies in his tummy to fuck off, Caleb knocked on the front door.

A short and dark-haired woman flung open the portal with gusto and a hollered, "Don't you dare get dirty. We are leaving for the picnic in a minute."

Orders given, Melanie turned to face Caleb and uttered an eloquent, "Oh."

"Hey, brat face." The old nickname came easily.

Still unable to find words, Melanie showed him her happiness at seeing him again by throwing her arms around him in a big hug.

"Good grief, are you sure you're not part anaconda?" he joked as she bound him tight.

"No one's too sure what great-great grandpa was, so you never know. But you didn't come here to hash out my ancestral lines, and since I know you already caught up with Daryl,"—Melanie drew herself out of his arms and peered up at him—"that means there's only one reason why you're here. Renny." Melanie hauled off and slugged him in the gut.

It didn't hurt, but it still made him exclaim, "What the hell? What happened to I'm glad to see you?"

"I am, but you also broke my best friend's heart. Do you know how hard she's had to struggle because you're an asshat?"

A cringe pulled his features taut. "I swear I didn't know about the baby. I just found out last night."

"Like fu—udge," Melanie said, stuttering her reply as a commotion at her feet drew her attention.

A pair of tousle-haired, dark-eyed boys stared up at him.

They didn't blink. Or move.

A waft of chocolate rose from one of them. With a sly grin, the slightly smaller of the two licked a sticky finger, not that it helped the brown smear on his hand. The little tyke regarded the cocoa smear, and

Melanie growled, "I thought I hid the chocolate syrup."

"Found it," announced the tyke with no small amount of pride.

"More like it found you," she muttered. "Don't you dare wipe it on your pants."

The little guy listened to his mother and found something else to latch his sticky hand onto.

Caleb didn't have time to move back because the child moved so fast. One minute, the kid looked like he would defy his mother, and the next, he flung his arms around Caleb's legs, peeked up, and grinned. "Hi."

"Holy sh—oot," he said, curbing his language at the last second. "How do you resist the cuteness?"

"You don't, which is why they're spoiled monsters. Tatum, let go of Caleb's leg." Tatum required Melanie leaning forward to pry him loose, but the damage was done. Caleb's jeans were smeared in chocolate. Melanie eyed the sticky spots. "Sorry about that. Terrible twos are nothing compared to the Terrifying threes."

"So these are your boys?" Caleb didn't wait for an answer to his obvious question. He crouched down and studied the faces.

Identical twins in all ways from the messy mop of hair to the solemn stares to the mischief pulling at their lips. If it weren't for the fact that Tatum was slightly smaller than his brother, Caleb didn't know how you'd tell them apart.

The one without chocolate-smeared hands held out his arms and commanded, "Up."

Caleb stood.

The child waved his arms again, and Melanie

laughed. "He didn't mean stand up. He meant pick him up. Looks like you've made a friend. That demanding fellow is Rory."

Making friends—even if cute and scary to hold, as the child clung to his upper body like a monkey—wasn't what Caleb came for.

"I need help," he blurted out.

"You're doing fine." Melanie said in a soothing tone. "Don't worry. They're practically impossible to drop now. They've got a grip like their mother. It's when they're babies you gotta watch out. One minute they're diaperless on the change table, peeing in the air while you're diving looking for a towel, and the next they're rolling in opposite directions and hitting the floor. Good thing they're tough, just like their daddy."

Andrew, tough? Caleb vaguely recalled slamming him into a locker a time or two. Which, in retrospect, was a bit of a dick move. But hey, that was high school.

"Yeah, so about that help. I have a son."

"His name is Luke," Melanie announced as she walked away and entered a living room.

Caleb followed, a monkey still on his hip. "You know him?"

"Duh." Melanie rolled her eyes. "I babysit him when Renny's at her day job."

Jackpot. If anyone could help him understand his son, Melanie could, because asking Renny was out of the question. "Perfect. I need pointers on being a dad."

Well, that got her gaping. "You mean you're planning to stay?"

"I think so. Maybe."

Her dark brows drew into a frown. "Maybe? That's not good enough. You are either in one hundred percent or you're out. That boy deserves better than to have his hopes raised, only to have them dashed."

"What if I swore to do my best?"

"What if I swore to hunt you down and geld you if you hurt my best friend and her son again?" So sweetly said, yet he caught the threatening thread underlying it.

"Deal." Because if he disappointed Renny, and now his son, Melanie wouldn't have to hurt him. He'd be dead.

Chapter Six

In her summer frock—bought on a clearance rack for a fraction of its price—Renny stood with Luke on the edge of the picnic currently in full swing behind the Bittech Institute.

I shouldn't have come.

She hadn't planned to come, but Melanie—using some kind of alien sixth sense—must have sensed Renny's plan to back out because she called and played Renny the world's tiniest violin.

"But you have to come, or I'm liable to go completely nutso on those uptight human wives of the other executives."

"Have you forgotten? I'm human," Renny retorted. She hadn't inherited her father's shifter gene, but Luke sure had an animal inside. Every now and then, his eyes would flash a vivid green and his irises would slit. What she would do when he shifted into his croc form, she didn't know. She couldn't exactly teach him what to do. The one person who could was the one she wanted to avoid.

A man she couldn't stop thinking about.

After the revelation the night before that Caleb had not even known about Luke, she'd struggled with her emotions. On the one side, she simmered with rage at the knowledge he'd destroyed her letters, and thus ignored their son. But, at the same time, she couldn't help a spurt of hope. Hope because she'd seen the genuine shock in his eyes when he heard of their son.

And admit it, a part of you has already forgiven him because at least now you know he didn't intentionally abandon our child.

Rewind and try to remember, though, that he did abandon you.

For that alone, she should never forgive him, and that would probably work a lot better if she could stop obsessing about him.

Her inability to keep him out of her thoughts proved to be the catalyst for her choice. Rather than stay home and deal with all the chores—and let her mind churn over what to do with Caleb—she chose to go to the picnic.

"Get dressed," she'd told Luke. "We are going on a picnic." Thing was, now that she was here, she wasn't sure she'd made the right choice in coming.

While dressed in her nicest, Renny still felt as if she stood out among the other women in their crisp pastel linens with their perfectly coiffed hair. Her flowered summer frock was almost as bad as Melanie's vivid red strapless summer gown with its high waist and frothy skirt.

A tingling awareness only gave her a second to brace herself before she heard a murmured, "Hey, baby."

Before Renny could reply, her son reacted, whirling to face Caleb, his little body bristling as he put himself between them. A soft growl rumbled from Luke, and she couldn't help her mouth rounding into an O of surprise.

"Luke. Stop that." She almost said, *Don't growl at*

your father. The sharp nip to her tongue stopped the words in time.

Even if Luke didn't understand who stood before him, Caleb did, and he sucked in a breath. He looked at her instead of their son, his expression torn, eyes full of panic, his breath coming fast. "So this is…"

"My son, Luke." No way was she confirming this was Caleb's son aloud, not with Luke listening. She wondered what Caleb was doing here and what he planned to do next.

Renny certainly never expected him to drop to his haunches and bring himself eye level with their son.

"Hey there, Luke. My name is Caleb." The big, scarred soldier, who outweighed Luke several times over, held out his hand, anxiety making him tense. Was it her or did his body tremble?

If the moment wasn't so emotionally charged, it would have made her smile.

No smiles. No softening. She had to remain strong. "What do you think you are doing?" Renny demanded.

"Introducing myself," Caleb said, never taking his eyes from their boy. The outstretched hand hung out there, and Luke appeared to ponder the offering before slowly slipping his smaller one into the grasp. Caleb shook it as if it was made of spun glass.

That made her laugh. "He's not going to break that easily."

"I'm tough." Luke puffed out his chest. "Because I'm the man of the house."

"You are?" Caleb replied lightly.

Luke nodded. "Mama said so on account I have no daddy. Rory and Tatum do. So do Philip and Cory."

Her son's unexpected talkativeness caused Caleb to blanch, and he might have squeezed a little too tight. Or her son sensed the weird vibe in the air. Either way, Luke yanked his hand away. "I wanna go play."

"Stay in sight," she admonished as Luke ran off and joined Melanie's boys, who were already leading their mother on a merry chase around the tables set with white linen and covered dishes.

"What are you doing here, Caleb? What are you trying to prove?" With Luke out of earshot, Renny didn't feel a need to temper her words.

"I'm not doing anything. Just thought I'd go to a picnic."

"You don't work for Bittech."

"Not currently. But Daryl was saying I should apply, seeing as how they're looking for more guys to beef up their security."

"If you're staying, then I am leaving."

She spun, meaning to grab her son and go, but Caleb stepped in front of her, a brick wall of muscle that once upon a time she would have snuggled.

"Running away, baby?"

She angled her chin. "Merely trying to avoid a scene. What happened to you staying away from me so it wouldn't be awkward?"

"I changed my mind."

Excuse me? "Well, change it back. You were right. This is awkward." And exhilarating. But most of all, it was scary, scary because she didn't really want to go.

He moved closer, and she automatically took a step back.

"Do I make you nervous?" he asked.

Caleb made her feel a lot of things. Nervous was among them, but maybe not for the reason he thought.

"I don't want anything to do with you. Was I not clear enough before?"

"You don't want to be seen with me. Can't say as I blame you. I'm definitely not as pretty as I used to be."

No, he wasn't, but he was definitely sexier, his boyish edge hardened by experience. The scars didn't take away from his attraction, merely showcased his toughness.

"I am not that shallow, Caleb. I really don't give a pickle what you look like, but I won't have you leading Luke on. He's got it tough enough as it is without you confusing matters."

"What's confusing about the fact I'm his father?"

"Not yet you aren't. That title has to be earned." Because she was damned if she was just going to let Caleb into her son's life without him proving he could handle it.

And he had to prove he wouldn't run off again.

Before Caleb could respond, she walked away, making a beeline for Melanie, who wore a plastered smile on her face and had a death grip on her water glass. A trio of wives surrounded Melanie, cutting off all escape.

Being a good friend, Renny plowed right on through with a murmured, "Excuse me, ladies, but I need to borrow my BFF here for a minute. Girl stuff." She yanked her friend away from the gaggle and, once they'd gone a few yards, stopped.

Melanie blew out a breath. "Thanks for saving

me. My inner kitty was really pushing me to sharpen my claws. I'm pretty sure the tall one to my left is made of plastic."

"Don't thank me yet. I'm mad at you. How could you tell Caleb I would be here?"

"That jerk. I can't believe he ratted me out," Melanie huffed.

"He didn't."

"You tricked me."

"Telling the truth isn't a trick, and it was easy to figure out since you were the only one who knew I was coming."

"Fine. So I told him where you'd be. What else was I supposed to do? He showed up at my place wearing a woebegone expression." Melanie jutted her lip and batted her eyes.

Renny snorted. "I don't care how sorry he looks. I'm not ready to deal with him yet."

"You never will be, which is why you need to suck it up. If not for your own peace of mind then Luke's."

"Nothing wrong with my mind." Most days.

"Except for the fact you never got over him."

"What are you talking about? I've dated other guys. Slept with a few, too." None that left a lasting impression, though.

"And how many lasted more than a few weeks?"

Try more than a few dates. "It's not my fault I'm picky."

An eloquent roll of her eyes was Melanie's initial reply. "Why not just admit none of them were the right guys?"

"I have no problem admitting it. I'll know it when I find the one."

"Or you'll deny it until you die a spinster of old age. God, you're stubborn."

"What are you implying?" Renny asked, even if she already knew.

"You are the Queen of De-Nile," Melanie said, the old joke not enough to tone down the seriousness of their talk. "I think that the reason you never moved on was because you'd already found the one."

"Are you talking about *Caleb*?" Renny's voice pitched.

"Are you pining after another guy I don't know about? Hell yeah, I'm talking about Caleb. Admit it, he's the one."

"*The one*"—and, yes, Renny finger quoted it as she said it—"left me without so much as a goodbye or a reason. And now he waltzes back into town and thinks he can say he is sorry and suddenly become a part of my life again."

"Hate to break it to you, girlfriend, but he already is a part of your life. He always will be because he's Luke's daddy."

Hard to argue that fact, so Renny went for diversion instead. "Speaking of daddies, there's Andrew with Rory under his arm, and he doesn't look very happy."

"When is he ever happy?" Melanie muttered.

Trouble in suburban paradise. As the best friend, Renny was privy to many secrets, one of them being the fact that things hadn't been right between Melanie and Andrew for a while. But Renny knew Melanie was doing her damnedest to change that. Was that where the plan for another kid came from?

"Want me to go save the boys?" Renny asked. She seriously meant save, too, because while Andrew might have donated sperm, his fathering skills left much to be desired.

"Too late. They got into the donuts." Tatum, lips powdered in white, his small hands, too, clutched at his father's dark slacks. White fingerprints marred the fabric. Melanie sighed. "Dammit. I better get Andrew's spare set of clothes before he has a fit."

"You travel with spares?" Renny asked.

"Spares?" Melanie snorted. "Try triplicates. I have twin demons of mischief. We're lucky if we only need two outfits a day. And Andrew is so finicky when it comes to being clean. I'll be back in a few."

Melanie teetered off in the direction of the parking lot, stopping halfway to slip off her heels.

Renny held back a smile. Her friend might have married upper middle class, but at heart, she was still a bayou girl, and preferred to go about barefoot.

Alone for the moment, Renny let her gaze rove until she located her son, only to discover Luke was being watched by Caleb, watched with a rapier gaze, and she noted how he clenched his fists instead of lunging when Luke tripped chasing Rory around a tree.

Caleb might hesitate to intervene, but she wouldn't. She went to his side, concern creasing her expression. "Are you all right, bug?"

Before Luke could burst into tears and make a drama about the green stain on his knee, a deep, gravelly voice interjected.

"Of course the boy is fine. He's tough. Anyone can tell just by looking at him. Must get it from his mother."

Renny might have chided Wes for his words, except one moment her son went from looking like he'd start wailing to puffing his chest out and boasting, "Didn't hurt at all."

And off went her boy, chasing the twins again.

A moue twisted her lips. "I can't believe that worked."

"He's a boy." Chauvinism, alive and well, and thriving in Wes Mercer.

Standing, Renny stroked her hand down her skirt to make sure it hung where it should before she took in Wes's appearance, a hard guy to miss. Nothing about the guy was small, from his bulging arms to his wide shoulders to the smirk on his lips.

"Something funny?" she asked.

"Other than the way you're mollycoddling your boy?" The dark arch of his brow spoke of his disdain.

"I am not smothering him. Much." Although hadn't Melanie accused her of over parenting? Actually, her exact words had been very similar to Wes's. *"He's a boy. He's supposed to jump off things."*

At least Wes didn't say the other thing Melanie had as well, *"He needs a father."* And Renny was looking for one. Kind of.

She noted Wes staring intently over her shoulder. "What are you looking at?"

A smile stretched his lips, not exactly a nice one. "Your ex-boyfriend is staring daggers at me right now."

"What did you do?"

"Me?" Wes failed at looking innocent. He'd been born bad. Bad genes. Bad upbringing. Bad boy. But sinfully handsome with his dark hair and tanned skin.

"Yes, you. I know how you like to taunt Caleb. You always have."

Wes's smile widened. "Can I help it if that croc snaps so easily?"

"Maybe if you didn't do it on purpose, he wouldn't freak."

"But here's the beauty. I actually wasn't trying to annoy him when I stopped to talk to you. However, I am so glad I did because he is practically bursting out of his skin. If he were a cat or a dog, he'd have already pissed on you to mark his territory."

Renny couldn't help a wrinkle of her nose. "That's just being gross. And you're wrong. I mean nothing to Caleb, so why would he care if another guy is talking to me?"

"Not just any guy. Me." Wes stepped closer, looming in her space, and for a moment, she wondered what was wrong with her.

Wes was hot. Like super attractive. Yet, even though he stood close to her, the scent of him clean and sharp, she wasn't in the least attracted.

It wasn't because she knew of his reputation as the boy to stay away from. Make that the one all the girls wanted.

He's hot. Which was why she couldn't understand, when he turned an intense gaze on her, which was only enhanced by the slight smirk on his lips, she hardly felt a thing. Mild interest at most.

Her lack of attraction made her bold. "Why didn't we ever hook up?" she asked.

She took him off balance—she could see by the widening of his eyes—but he had a ready retort.

"Because you were dating Caleb."

"And after?"

"You left."

She rolled her eyes. "And I came back. This is like, what, the third time we've run into each other? Each time you do a little flirt, and yet you've never asked me out."

"I don't like to waste my time. Any idiot can see you're still pining for Caleb."

"I am not."

"Really? Then prove it." The smile that tugged Wes's lips held a challenge no one could resist. Not even her.

Because I have not been pining for Caleb. She could and would date whoever she wanted. Even a Mercer!

"You're on."

Leaning on tiptoe, she heard Wes murmur, "Oh, this is going to create some chaos."

Maybe it would. Maybe it would throw Caleb into a tizzy, but that was okay. It was about time he got some payback for leaving her.

Let him feel something. Let him realize just what he'd lost.

Renny's lips met Wes's, and there was no electrical spark, no kaboom of the senses. It was…nice.

It thankfully didn't last long.

"I hope I'm not interrupting." The right words, but given Caleb spat them out through gritted teeth, not all that pleasant.

Renny pulled away from Wes, only to stiffen at the possessive hand Caleb dared place on the middle of her back. The fabric of her dress prevented skin-to-skin contact, and yet, awareness ignited in her.

Gosh darn it. An actual kiss did nothing, but Caleb thinking he could claim her in public had her wetting her panties.

It wasn't fair. She tried to move away from his touch, sidestepping left then right. Caleb simply followed her, never relinquishing his claim.

His stubbornness didn't endear him to her in the least. "Hands off," she hissed over her shoulder.

Caleb completely ignored her, focusing instead on Wes. "If it isn't my old school chum."

"Chum? I believe the trending word these days is frenemies. How have you been, snaggletooth? Did you run and leave behind a whole other bunch of people before coming here?"

At Wes's audacity, Renny sucked in a breath.

The tension in Caleb rose a notch. His jaw hardened. "I didn't run. I served my time with the military and left with an honorable discharge."

"Ah yes. The military. Can't say as I ever felt the urge. I much preferred to stay behind and enjoy the benefits of home." Renny bit her lip instead of giggling as Wes winked, so obviously baiting Caleb.

Caleb, though, didn't think Wes joked. "Stay away from Renny."

Jealousy. Oh my, there was no denying it. Caleb was jealous. A spurt of warmth curled low in her body. *No. Don't give in.*

Fight the attraction. Fight it with anger. "You can't decide who I see." This time, she managed to completely evade Caleb's touch and stood apart from both men, arms crossed over her chest.

Wes outright laughed. "You've been told. Hope you don't lose too much sleep thinking about how badly you'll fare when she compares me against you."

His smug assurance irritated her, too. "You might be cute, Wes, but I am not interested in dating a sexist thug."

"Thug?" Wes arched a brow. "I haven't had an arrest since I turned eighteen."

"Doesn't mean you're walking the straight and narrow," Caleb pointed out. "Every one knows the Mercers are dirty."

Wes lost his happy smile. "Maybe everyone should pay more attention before casting out insults. Now, while it's been just fucking grand catching up, I'm going to have to ask you what you're doing here."

But Caleb just flipped the query around. "What are you doing here?"

"I'm here as part of the security detail for this party."

Something Renny had known, but she could see how Caleb might not have, especially since Wes was dressed just like one of the guests. Dark slacks, a dark mauve button-up shirt, the material filmy and light, and a dark gray tie.

"You're a guard?" Caleb let loose a derisive snort. "Isn't that kind of like letting the gator into the henhouse? Also, since when does a Mercer have a real job? What, did you run out of contraband to smuggle? Lost the recipe for your grandpa's moonshine?"

Rather than flaring Wes's temper, Caleb's outburst served only to bring back his cool smirk. "I see serving time with the military didn't improve your sense of humor. And being a veteran doesn't give you an automatic invite to this party. I'm going to have to ask you to leave."

"Melanie invited me."

"Ask me if I give a fuck. I'll bet if I ask her husband, he'll tell me to kick your ass out to the curb." Wes sounded quite confident, and Renny had a feeling Andrew wouldn't side with Caleb. One too many swirlies in high school.

"Andrew always was a whiny dick who couldn't do shit for himself."

Renny winced at Caleb's insult, yet couldn't quite disagree. Personally, she'd always thought Melanie could do better. But then again, her friend technically had, seeing as how she was the one married and living in a real house.

But speaking of Andrew drew Renny's attention to something. "Melanie's not back yet with Andrew's change of clothes."

Surely she'd had enough time to get to the parking lot and back. A vague sense of wrongness made Renny gnaw her lower lip.

"She probably got stopped for a chat."

"Maybe. I'm still going to go find her. It's time I grabbed Luke and headed out anyhow."

"I'll walk you to your car," Caleb offered.

Before she could say, "No, thank you," a murmur rose in the crowd. Even before someone held aloft a familiar pair of heels—only Melanie would wear black stilettos to a picnic—Wes was moving, his hand dropping to his side to grab at a two-way radio.

He pressed the button. "Teams A and B, missing female, five-foot-nothing, in a bright red gown..."

The detail Wes conveyed proved quite elaborate. The man had an eye for detail? Or had he just noticed

Melanie?

There was a time in high school when Renny wondered if her friend would date him. The bad boy every mother hated. But Melanie had chosen to be more mature about her choice. Andrew was going places. Andrew was a gentleman.

Andrew also bored the heck out of Melanie. But she still chose him.

From the strand of trees yards away to their left, the twins burst forth, wailing. Standing with his mouth gaping, Andrew did nothing to calm them, leaving Renny to run and gather them into her arms in an attempt to calm them.

"Shh. Calm down and tell me what's wrong."

Rory sobbed. "A dinosaur got mama."

"It's probably gonna eat her." Tatum sniffled.

"What is? Did you see something?"

Matching tousled heads nodded. "A monster," they announced in chorus, but that was all they would say. That and a small voice saying, "It was scary."

"You're safe now," Renny murmured, tucking them close. "I promise there are no monsters or dinosaurs roaming around. I'll bet your mom is just fine, you'll see."

Despite her reassurance, the twins' fear proved contagious, and Renny peeked for her son, cursing herself for not having grabbed him, too. What if something did roam in the bayou?

Something stalked all right, but it was on two legs and had a hand on her son's shoulder.

The look that trusting Luke turned on Caleb wrenched something in her, and she couldn't help but shiver, unable to ignore the ominous portent.

For the first time she understood why Wanda liked to say, "Someone's plotting against us. Get the gun."

Chapter Seven

The moment someone held aloft those shoes, Caleb came to life.

Danger. Stand on guard.

Given the way Caleb suffered from anxiety, you'd think that a whiff of danger would send him into a fit.

Yet, this was the odd thing about Caleb's psyche issues. Danger always seemed to energize him. It drew his scaly beast. The one he fought to keep hidden, except in times like these when alarm bells went off. He needed the predator to assess the situation.

First thing, where were Renny and Luke? She was easy to spot, her arms slipping around Melanie's wailing twins, but Luke wasn't with her. Pivoting around, Caleb didn't have to turn far to find his son.

The small lad, less than half his size, stood right beside him. A little hand slipped into his, and for once, Caleb didn't flinch at the unexpected contact.

His son might not know yet who he was, but he trusted Caleb to protect him.

He trusts me. Even if he had no reason to. Something in Luke recognized Caleb. Understood Caleb provided safety.

"Will you help find Aunt Melanie?" The murmured request took Caleb by surprise.

"There's already people looking for her."

"But not in the right place. They're looking in the building."

"Of course they're checking there first because Melanie probably went to the ladies room or something." Except why drop her shoes on the edge of the pavement, coincidentally just around the curve of the building where no one from the party could see anything? And why would the twins have come running from the woods screaming?

"The thing in the swamp took her."

"Thing? What thing?" Caleb turned a sharp gaze down at his son, who stared off at the vegetation bordering the cleared field.

"A dinosaur."

For a moment, his first impulse was to scoff, and yet for some reason, Caleb instead asked, "What makes you think it was a dinosaur?"

"It was green and scaly."

"So maybe you saw a crocodile or an alligator. They might seem like dinosaurs."

Holy fuck, his son could roll his eyes like a pro. "I know what a croc and gator look like. And they don't walk on two legs."

Not usually, but the time Caleb had spent in the military, away from what he knew and immersed in a world where the mysteries of magic weren't lost, he'd seen things. Impossible things. He'd met impossible shifters. Men who shifted only partially, sporting the heads of jackals. Stallions, with the upper torsos of men, the centaurs of old. Then the scariest thing of all, the naga, a beast thought hunted to extinction. The serpentine monster wasn't dangerous because of its deadly strength, but because of the poisonous nature of their voice. Whatever the naga asked, a person did. He should know. He'd suffered under the influence of one for much too long. His scar tightened. Fire had severed that slave-like bond.

These experiences meant Caleb was well aware the world was much more vast and varied than most people, even shifters, imagined. It meant he kept his mind open to the possibility of a gator or even a croc walking about on two legs.

"Did the thing have two arms as well?" Caleb asked.

A nod of his son's head. "With claws. And its face was weird."

Face, not muzzle or snout. Interesting choice of word.

Caleb kept a hold of Luke's hand as Renny made her way to him, the twins now clinging to their father—who seemed vastly uncomfortable—confronted with his children's hiccupping sobs.

What a useless tool, but not Caleb's problem.

When Renny got close enough, he asked, "Did the boys mention anything to you after they came out of the woods?"

"As a matter of fact, they did. Something about a monster."

"A dinosaur," Luke corrected.

"Yes, one of them said that. Probably a reptile of some kind that scared them, but I can't see Melanie getting taken unawares by one."

He couldn't disagree. As part of the feline Pantherinae family, even in her human form, Melanie had a very developed sense of smell.

"I don't suppose you've heard of a two-legged

lizard man roaming in the swamp?"

A brow arched as Renny stared at him. "Is this your way of insulting Wes again? The Mercers aren't at fault for everything. And, besides, he was standing with us when she went missing."

A clamor went up from the far end of the clearing, where a weeping willow draped the shore to the creek in a thick curtain. From between the strands, a man in a purple shirt appeared carrying something crimson.

Renny squinted, but not for long, as Caleb, with his better eyesight, spoke aloud, "It's Wes, and it looks like he's got Melanie."

"Is she all right?" A fair question to ask since her friend was being carried instead of walking.

A moment later, she got her answer as a shrill shriek shot across the field. "How dare you!"

"I wonder what Wes did this time."

"He's a Mercer. Does it matter?" was Caleb's reply as he watched a throng of people descend on Melanie and her rescuer. "You wanna go check on her?"

Before he'd even finished asking, she was striding towards Melanie, she just never made it anywhere close to her side as a cluster of hens, dressed in pastels, swarmed her best friend with a bevy of questions.

"Oh my God, you're alright."

"What happened?"

"Is it true you were abducted by a dinosaur?"

And a lowly murmured, "Attention slut."

While Caleb towered high enough to see what happened, Renny had to rely on peeks in between the milling bodies, not that there was much to see. Melanie was still in Wes's grip, the Bittech guard for some reason not setting her down or passing her off, probably because Andrew was too busy off to the side whispering in his phone.

Asshat. A true mate would be more worried about his wife.

Catching her best friend's eye, Renny pantomimed a phone to her ear and mouthed, "Call me later."

Melanie mouthed back, "Save me."

Eyeing the chatterboxes having a marvelous time practicing their drama, Renny shook her head.

Caleb couldn't help but smirk. "Aren't you going to wade in there and rescue her?"

"No way am I diving between those hens and their moment." Instead of rescuing Melanie, Renny waved and mouthed. "Bye."

No mistaking the lip synching of "Bitch. I hate you."

"I think you peeved her off," Caleb stated.

Renny laughed. "Good. It's payback for that last blind date Melanie sent me on. How she ever thought that visiting scientist who still lived with his mother would appeal, I will never figure out." Turning around, Renny began to walk in the direction of the parking lot.

Caleb stuck to her side and said, "Are you sure you don't want to stay and talk to Melanie, and make sure she's fine?"

Renny shook her head. "There's too many *people*"—she inclined her head to the human contingent—"for us to really talk. She seems okay now, so I'm just going to take Luke home."

"Let me walk you to your car."

"You don't have—"

Caleb held up hand. "Don't even start. Melanie just went missing. We don't know why. Her boys and Luke claim they saw something. Now is not the time to let your dislike of me prevent you from doing the right thing."

"I can protect Mommy from the dinosaur."

They both looked down at Luke, who, despite his brave words, looked pale.

A sigh escaped Renny. "Fine. You can walk with us, but I warn you, I'm parked at the back of the lot. Fashionably late means terrible parking."

"I know. I'm by the dumpster." Caleb shuddered. "I forgot to hold my breath when I got out of the truck."

Luke giggled.

They both peeked down, and Caleb saw Luke staring at him. "You're funny," the little boy said. No mistaking the shine of hero worship.

It didn't take a genius for Caleb to understand the scowl Renny sent his way. He shrugged. It wasn't as if he'd done it on purpose to make his son like him.

And he damn sure wouldn't take it back.

As Luke skipped only a few paces ahead, confident in the fact that he had someone watching his back, Caleb muttered in a low tone, "Why so pissed?"

"You're on the scene like, what, twenty minutes, and he's looking at you like you're some kind of demigod."

"The boy isn't doing this to hurt your feelings."

"I know that, but it doesn't mean it's fair, or not hurtful. I do everything for him and have to fight for even a smile these days. He hands it to you for doing nothing but existing and telling a dumb joke." Her lower lip jutted.

"So you're mad because our son likes me?"

Judging by the scowl she turned his way, yes.

"Do you know I am not even allowed to kiss him on the cheek anymore when I drop him off at school?" She clamped her lips as Luke skipped back and tucked his hand into Caleb's.

"There's our car," the boy announced.

Which meant there wasn't much time left.

Caleb couldn't just let her drive off. Could he? So many things crowded the air between them, and perhaps she sensed it because she handed Luke her car keys. "Bug, can you do Mommy a favor and open the windows so we don't die of the heat?"

With a high-pitched, "Yes," his son zipped off, keys jangling in his fist.

"He seems so small," Caleb noted in the sudden silence.

"Funny, because to me he seems so big now. He's healthy and just the right size for his age."

"You've done a good job, Renny. He seems like a great kid."

A heavy sigh left her. "I know. He's the best, but he is missing one thing in his life. Something I can't give him."

"What? Tell me and I'll get it."

"Can you?" She stopped walking and turned to give him a serious expression. "Because what Luke really needs most of all is a father."

"I thought you wanted me to stay away." Not that he thought he could. Now that Caleb had met his son, he was more determined than ever to stick around.

"Apparently, my brilliant plan to hold off on telling Luke about his father was doomed to failure. Even though I haven't said a thing, anyone can see he's drawn to you."

Like knew like.

"So what does that mean?" He didn't dare make any assumptions.

"It means I wish I was a big bad B-word. Because only a big B would keep a son from his father."

He couldn't help but grin. "Is this your cute way of saying bitch?"

She cringed. "You didn't have to say it aloud."

"Sorry, baby."

"And stop with the baby thing, Caleb. We're not a couple anymore. Just because I think you should spend time with Luke—"

"You do?"

"Yes, I do. But that decision doesn't mean I've forgiven you or that things are okay between us."

Yet.

But I'm going to change that, baby.

This was one mission he wouldn't fail.

Arriving at her car, Caleb frowned. While the body was in decent shape, anyone could tell the car was worn. The tires didn't match, and the tread left on them wasn't deep enough to provide real traction. "Please don't tell me you actually drive this thing?"

"I'll have you know this thing gets me where I need to go. Most of the time," she added under her breath.

"It's got roll down windows." Incredulity

colored his tone.

"And no air conditioning. Something about no more freezer thingy stuff in the lines. But it's not a big deal."

"You've got duct tape on the seats."

"With pretty little duckies on it. Are you done insulting my car now?"

"No." A smile split Caleb's lips. "But I can save some for later."

"Speaking of later, maybe you'd like to come over later." She slapped a hand over her mouth as soon as she said it.

Before she could retract, he accepted right away. "Sounds like a plan."

Watching, he stood as few yards away as she started the car and reversed it out of the spot. He was close enough to hear her mutter, "What the hell did I just do?"

But even more heartening were his son's words. "I'm going to show him my DS when he comes."

And Caleb would show them he was a man they could rely on. A man who wouldn't run. Never again.

Only once Renny was on her way did Caleb feel some of his tension ease. The woman he never stopped loving and his son were away from the danger.

Yet his beast didn't settle down. On the contrary, it pushed at the bindings that held it. Pushed. And pushed.

Caleb snarled. *Stop fighting. I am not letting you out.*

For distraction, he glanced to see what happened with the picnic. Caleb noted Melanie striding to the Bittech building, her twins clinging to her hands. Her husband walked a few paces ahead of her, busy on his phone. However, Daryl's sister was of less interest than Wes, who stood at the edge of the paved drive and stared into the woods.

What was he looking for? And more importantly, did it threaten Renny and Luke?

"So which of your cousins played a prank on the boss's wife?" he asked, coming up behind Wes.

The other man didn't turn. "It wasn't one of us. My family knows better than to lay a hand on her."

An odd statement to make. Melanie was in no way related to the Mercers, so why would Wes infer Melanie was protected?

Picking on one of the Mercers, especially one of Wes's siblings, meant bringing a shitload of trouble down on your head. Wes took his job as oldest in his family very seriously. He'd started stealing from a young age to help feed all the mouths, especially once his dad got injured and couldn't smuggle drugs through the bayou no more.

But don't feel sorry for the bastard. Wes might have a strong sense of family, but he was a dick. Belonging to the reptile family didn't mean they got along. On the contrary, their rivalry was legend, especially when it came to hunting in the bayou.

Speaking of hunting, nothing he'd ever tracked smelled as odd as the faintly lingering scent emanating from the direction of the woods. "What is that stench? Or is that your cologne?"

"Do you mean your mom's perfume?" Wes smirked. "On the other hand, if you're talking about that funky smell coming from the woods, then I don't know, but whatever it is, Melanie reeked of it."

"Where did you find her anyhow?"

"Under the willow tree, on the other side where no one could see her. Sleeping like a fucking princess."

"That makes no sense. How did she get there?"

"She doesn't know, and all I found was that smell…" Wes trailed off. "But you didn't stick behind to ask me about some kind of bayou creature. What do you want?"

"Just so we're clear, I'm back to stay."

Wes tossed him a hard look. "Is that supposed to be a warning?"

"Luke is my son."

"About time you claimed him."

"You knew?"

Wes shrugged. "Not at first, but when I saw the two of you side by side… No mistaking that giant square head. My condolences to Renny's snatch."

A growl vibrated through him. "Watch your mouth. I'm warning you right now, I don't want you near my son, and stay away from Renny."

"Isn't that up to her?"

"No!" The word burst from him and Wes arched a brow.

"I wonder what she'll say when she finds out. And just so you know, I have no interest in your girl. I just like to jab at your thick hide."

"Well, jab at someone else. I gotta enough working against me in winning over Renny. I don't need you mucking around fucking shit up."

"You can have Renny."

"How magnanimous of you." Caleb's sarcasm dripped.

"Not really, more like selfish interest. She's got a kid, and that means she needs someone stable. I ain't ready to settle down."

"Now if only more Mercers would think the same way and keep it in their pants."

"Says the guy with a bastard."

The bruised knuckles as Caleb replied to that statement?

Totally worth it.

Chapter Eight

Was the price of her sanity worth letting Caleb into her life? By the time Renny had reached home, she still wasn't sure. Doing the right thing for her son wasn't necessarily the right thing for her. Being near Caleb tested every ounce of her willpower. Did she have the strength to resist?

She feared the answer.

Confused and anxious, she put a call in to Melanie, only to have it go right to voicemail. It made her wonder if perhaps she should have stayed.

Then we could have spent more time with Caleb.

A Caleb who might be coming over later. Eek. What was she thinking?

She waited fifteen minutes before trying Melanie again.

The call was answered with, "Some best friend you are, leaving me to the tender mercy of those harpies."

"I would have stayed, but—"

"Instead preferred traipsing off with a long-lost soldier. That's fine, ditch your best friend for a hot guy. I get it. Did you finally give him a proper welcome home?"

Heat invaded Renny's cheeks and made her sputter. "I did not sleep with him."

"Yet."

"Never." Okay, that was a lie. It was more like yet, but only if he managed to wear down her resistance. Renny didn't want to get involved. Now if she could just convince the rest of her body to listen. "And why would you think I slept with him?"

"I saw you heading off with him and Luke."

"As protection. With the boys claiming they saw a dinosaur and you disappearing, he was just being cautious. He didn't want to see his son getting hurt."

"Sure he was."

"Fine. Don't believe me. But who cares about me? What in blue blazes happened to you?"

"Renny, such language." Melanie snickered into the phone. "As to what the fuck happened, your guess is as good as mine. One minute I'm walking to the car to get some pants, the next, bam, nothing."

Renny paced her small kitchen, keeping her voice low so that Luke wouldn't hear her. However, keeping it quiet proved hard, given Melanie's story. "What do you mean you don't remember anything after walking away from me? Surely you saw someone or something?"

"Nothing, just a great big blank until Wes planted one on me."

Shock stopped her nervous movement. "He kissed you while you were passed out?"

"That's what I call it, but he claims it was mouth to mouth."

"Do you believe him?" Renny asked.

"Of course not. He's a Mercer."

"Snob." Renny snickered. "Gosh, who would have expected you to ever become one."

"Shut up. I am not a snob. Merely discerning,"

Melanie declared in her snootiest voice.

Arching a brow, Renny snorted. "Is that what you're going with?"

"Fine. I'm a bitch. But let's look at facts. Apart from Wes, name one other Mercer with a real job?"

"Bruno."

"He's only a third cousin. He doesn't count."

"So did you?"

"Did I what?" Melanie asked.

"Kiss him back, of course," Renny asked.

"Renny! How could you ask that?"

"Because once upon a time you had the hots for each other in high school."

"And then I smartened up."

Yeah, her best friend had chosen stable and boring over sexy. Then again, who was Renny to criticize? She'd gone after the sexy bad boy and look where it had gotten her. "So are you telling me you didn't smooch him back at all?"

"It was totally one-sided. I'm a married woman."

"Who has to schedule sex with her husband."

"It's not Andrew's fault stress at work is killing his mojo. No matter how hot Wes is, I won't betray my vows. Now drop the subject, or I am going to start grilling you about Caleb."

"Nothing to talk about."

"Liar. Spill."

"Okay, so you'll be ecstatic to know that I'm going to tell Luke Caleb's his dad."

"You haven't done that yet?" Melanie screeched.

Renny winced. "I'm working on it. It's not easy

to announce to your kid, hey, Daddy's back in town and says he wants to get to know you."

"He does?"

At the little voice from behind her, Renny's eyes widened. She whirled, but sure enough, her son was no longer in the other room watching television from like ten inches away from the screen.

Nope. He'd ghosted to a spot behind her and heard...how much?

"Melanie, I gotta go. Crisis to handle over here." Renny hung up her phone as her son studied her.

"Hi, bug. How much did you hear?" In other words, could she chicken out of the truth for a while longer?

Nope.

"Caleb's my daddy," Luke announced. "I heard you say so to Auntie Mel."

She could only nod.

"Cool. I'm gonna show him my room, too, when he comes over."

And with that, her son turned around and wandered back to his spot just inches from the screen.

He sat still, legs in a lotus position, elbows on his knees, totally focused on the cartoons.

"Um, did you want to ask me any questions?" she asked.

For some reason, she expected the silent treatment, maybe a few accusations, but little boys handled things differently from adults. Luke turned to her and said, "What's for supper?"

With those words, she felt a flutter of panic. She'd invited Caleb over, but never specified a time.

Or given him an address, but that he could find

easily enough. Her traitor of a friend had probably programmed it into his GPS.

He could show up anytime, and given he was a guy, he'd want food. Heck, she wanted food. What a pity her kitchen held none.

Dragging a complaining Luke, she fled to the grocery store. She dawdled up and down the aisles, taking way too much time to decide what she wanted. Her budget could only stretch so far, but she didn't want Caleb to think she'd invited him over to guilt him on how they lived.

She eyed the packages of meat in the refrigerated display. So expensive, but she couldn't exactly expect him to be content with a salad and hot dog.

Steak it was, a big, thick one that cost more than she usually spent in a week on meat, and figuring what the hell, she grabbed a smaller one for herself and Luke to share. By the time she'd gathered some fresh vegetables and splurged on a premade dessert, it was almost five o'clock and closing time.

Small towns didn't keep the same hours as the city. Out here, once the sun started to go down, which was fairly early in the late fall, businesses closed, traffic slowed, and people hid in their homes—so the animals could come out and play.

Bitten Point was a shifter friendly town. Sure, it had its fair share of humans—they were after all the dominant race on the planet—however, those that chose to live there knew the secret. And if they didn't, they didn't stay long. There were ways to convince people it was best to move on.

Having grown up among the shifters, Renny

certainly didn't fear them, even when they wore their animal shape. A shifter crocodile or bear was no more likely to attack than when they sported their human guise. Only nature's unenlightened hunted, those who walked on two legs, and that was rare. Most wild creatures preferred to go after easy prey.

So when her son said, "Mama, there's something hiding at the edge of the woods," she didn't pay too much mind. Children had vivid imaginations. Heck, Melanie took the doors off her sons' closet so that the boogieman would stop hiding in there at night. As for Luke, Renny got him a bed with built-in drawers underneath so the monster under the bed wouldn't grab him.

The grocery story just outside of town, with its heavy discounts and clearance bins, bordered the swamplands. While quieter this cool time of the year, the area, with its lush vegetation, still hummed with life, some of it probably intimidating for a little boy.

She tossed the groceries in her trunk and slammed it shut. Only once she slid in her car and spoke to an empty back seat, "Are you buckled in, buddy?" did she realize Luke wasn't in the car. Out she jumped, heart hammering. "Luke? Luke? Where are you?"

"I see something." The faint reply had her scanning the area until she spotted her son standing on the crumbling concrete curb meant to hold the bayou back.

The little bug had wandered. "Come back here. Right this instant."

"Do I have to?" Luke turned with a sulk on his face. "I want to see."

97

Time to go into mommy mode. Renny planted her hands on her hips. "Now."

"Fine." As he huffed the word, he took two steps, and Renny felt all her breath whoosh as something dark swung from the shadows behind him, just missing his little body.

"Luke! Run!" She screamed the words as she darted toward him, but someone else was faster. A big body barreled past her and scooped a frantic-eyed Luke.

Renny pounded toward Caleb and her son, eyes darting between them and the shadows that no longer moved.

"What was that?" she asked, holding her arms out for her son, and while he clung for a moment to Caleb, in the end, Luke reached for her.

For the moment, Mommy still came first.

She hugged him close to her, eyes closed, trying to calm her racing heart.

"I didn't see anything. I heard your scream and came bolting around the corner."

"I thought I saw something in the woods." An admission that had her eyeing the shadows, and seeing nothing. Had she imagined it?

"Thought you saw…?"

"It was another one of the dinosaurs," Luke confided in a soft whisper. "They escaped."

"What are you talking about? Dinosaurs don't exist." Renny said it, and yet, it didn't emerge very convincing, especially given how pensive Caleb appeared.

"Even if they did, I don't want you to worry about any dinosaurs when I'm around, big guy. I was in the army, and we soldiers know how to take care of overgrown lizards."

"Says the biggest lizard of all," she muttered under her breath.

"The biggest, baby." The low growl of his reply tingled her skin with awareness. She tossed her head, still determined to keep him at arm's length.

But she couldn't do the same for Luke, who wiggled free from her grip. Setting him on the ground, she couldn't help a twinge as her heart swelled and at the same time shrank at her son's instinctive move to stand by his father's side.

Already he's feeling that bond to his father. It shouldn't have hurt, but it did.

"What are you doing here?" she asked. Either Caleb had uncanny timing, or he was stalking her. Funny how neither option bothered her, not like the fear of losing her son did.

"I wasn't sure what time you wanted me over, so I thought I'd grab some food before popping in on you. But…" He shot a look at the store and grimaced. "I arrived too late."

She would have said just in time. What if the thing she'd seen had not run off at Caleb's arrival? Would it have snatched her son like it had nabbed Melanie?

If it's even the same thing, you ninny.

Still, what were the chances of two occurrences of supposed dinosaurs happening in the same day?

"I've got food in my trunk. If you want to follow me," she offered.

"I don't suppose I could ask for a ride. My brother dropped me off because he needed his truck

99

tonight."

"Sure." She could handle the short ride from here to her place. This was a chance to prove Caleb's proximity didn't bother her. She could handle it.

Liar.

As soon as she slid behind the wheel, she noted her hands were shaking. Caleb noticed, too. "Are you sure you're okay?"

"Fine. Just fine." She sighed. "No. No, I'm not. Do you mind driving?"

He didn't question her shakiness. Probably blamed it on her recent fright, and yet the truth was, she felt like a teenager all over again around him. Tongue-tied, hyper aware, and high-strung. She didn't know if she'd scream if he touched her or would melt into a puddle.

Either way, was it perverse to want to find out?

As she switched sides, she peeked in to see Luke buckled in his booster seat, his gaze intent on Caleb.

Apparently, her son's little mind had been churning with questions because one popped free. "Are you really a soldier?"

"I was." Caleb glanced into the rearview mirror to look at their son. "I left Bitten Point a long time ago and fought in a war overseas."

"Did you kill people?"

"Luke! That is not an appropriate question." While Renny didn't mind a healthy curiosity, she drew the line at morbid.

Caleb placed a hand on her knee, an intimate gesture that sucked away any further protest, especially once she realized Caleb wasn't bothered. "I don't mind answering. I did kill some people. It's what soldiers do.

We go to war and do what we're told." So grimly said.

"Is the war how you got hurt?"

Renny could have moaned in embarrassment. "Luke, you shouldn't pry like that." Even if he asked some of the questions she'd wondered.

"It happened during my last mission. I got burned in a fire, a big one in a place where I was held prisoner."

"Someone captured you?" It was her turn to blurt out a query.

For a moment, she thought he wouldn't answer. His jaw locked, and his fingers gripped the wheel of her steering column so tightly his knuckles turned white. "Yes. I was a slave for a while to a..." Caleb trailed off as his eyes noted Luke's intent gaze in the mirror. "A really bad person."

"Did you kill them?"

"No." Stark. Flat. "But fear not, that person won't be bothering anyone else ever again. The good guys won the day."

The building Renny called home loomed, and she derailed the serious talk by pointing and saying, "This is our place." She waited for his derision, but Caleb simply pulled to the curb and turned off the motor.

Luke led the way up the outside steps to the apartment they had over the store.

Renny was empty-handed but for her keys, Caleb having insisted on bringing the groceries in. How domestic of him.

As a matter of fact, the next few hours were a surreal vision of what kind of life they could have had if he'd not abruptly left her.

While not a cook—unless catching a bass and spitting it over a fire in the bayou counted—Caleb was helpful in chopping up vegetables while answering questions from Luke, who it seemed had suddenly turned into a chatterbox.

"What's your favorite color?"

"Black."

"Mine is blue. What's your favorite chip? I like ketchup."

"Barbecue."

And on it went. Nothing as intense as the questions in the car, and a good thing, too, because Renny was having a hard enough time keeping her balance without getting caught up in Caleb's past.

Sitting at the small table as they ate almost choked her. *This is what families do, eat together, talk, laugh.*

She kept having to remind herself this wasn't real. Not permanent. Caleb might be there for the moment, but there was no guarantee he would stay.

As the hour drew late, Luke couldn't hide a yawn. Renny said, "Time for bed. Say goodnight to Caleb."

Her son shook his head. "Don't want to go. Wanna stay talking to my daddy."

The moment froze. Renny couldn't have said who was more stunned by Luke's use of the word daddy. Actually, given the fact that Caleb's eyes looked bright—*is he crying?*—she knew who.

It wasn't easy—a part of her screamed, *No, he's mine, how can you waltz in and steal him from me?*—but this wasn't about her. "Caleb, why don't you tuck Luke into bed? Make sure he brushes his teeth first, though."

"I wanna story, too," Luke demanded. Another

ritual passed on to the newcomer. But it was only one night, and could she blame her son for wanting this time with his father?

Yes. I raised him. And she was raising him right, which was why Renny pointed to her cheek. "Caleb can read to you, but I'm gonna need my goodnight kiss now then."

Luke ran to her and threw out his arms. She swept him into her embrace and plastered him with noisy kisses until he screeched and squirmed. "Mommy!"

Setting him down, she watched as Luke then crossed to Caleb and snagged his hand. "Come see my room." As their son tugged him away, Caleb tossed her a look over his shoulder and mouthed, "Thank you."

She turned away, lest he see the tears in her eyes. Not tears of anger that her son had chosen Caleb over her, but over what could have been.

While a part of her desperately wanted to spy on them, she let them have their alone time. If, and that was a big if, Caleb was serious about becoming a part of Luke's life, there would be plenty of opportunities to share bedtime and other things.

Supper dishes cleared away, she had time to sit on the couch before Caleb emerged from the bedroom. "He fell asleep before I was done with the story. I guess I was boring."

"He always does when I read, too."

"He called me daddy." Caleb said it, not able to hide his stunned tone.

"Because you are."

"But I don't know how to be one. What if I fuck up?" No mistaking the fear in those words.

"Welcome to the parenting club. You can read all the books you like and listen to all kinds of advice, but what it comes down to is just plain winging it."

That startled a laugh out of him. "Winging it?"

"It's worked for me so far, so don't be so quick to knock it." A silence fell between them, and she couldn't hold his gaze. "I guess you're going to head out now." Because Luke wasn't there to act as buffer anymore. It was just him and her—and some excitable hormones screaming, *Do something.*

"Do you want me to leave?"

A question fraught with undertones and, in her mind, a cop-out. "Yes." She didn't miss the flash of hurt in his eyes, which was why she sighed and added, "No. How's that for a clear answer?"

A smile creased his lips, a smile meant just for her. It affected her more than it should have. Warmth curled in her belly.

Caleb still had yet to move from in front of the bedroom door. He cast a glance around, and a frown creased his brow.

"Where's your bedroom?"

"You're standing in it."

"But there's no bed."

"Brilliant powers of observation." Sarcasm slid from her lips but without malice. Most people displayed the same shock when they found out her living situation. "Luke needed a bedroom with a door since he goes to sleep earlier, and this way his toys aren't all over the place."

"You guys could use a bigger place."

"A bigger place means more dollars." Then Renny hastened to add before he thought she was looking for a handout, "We're doing just fine here."

Caleb's lips pressed into a tight line. "Would you stop doing that?"

"Doing what?"

"Getting all prickly anytime I say anything about your life."

"Maybe I'm prickly because you seem awfully critical for a guy who just walked back into it. I'm doing the best I can." To her horror, her voice cracked.

Before she could realize what had happened, Caleb had leapt over the couch and drawn her into his arms. For a moment, she allowed him to hold her, savoring the feel of his body against hers, reveling in the touch of a man. This man.

Fire licked her senses, rousing them, and raising her temperature.

It would be so easy to tilt her face and find his lips.

So easy to succumb…

Yet so hard to recover if he hurt her again.

There was only one thing to do to destroy the intimacy building between them. She swiped her wet eyes and cheeks from side to side on his shirt and then, for good measure, honked her nose in it.

Chapter Nine

She didn't just do that.

Oh, but Renny had. She'd blown her tear-stuffed nose on him and then pulled back, a tiny smirk of triumph hovering at the corners of her lips.

Why would she do that? Renny was a lady, albeit a tough one given her upbringing, but still not one to be gross…unless she had an ulterior motive?

She moved away from him, heading for the box of tissues on the counter.

By the time she'd turned around, he was leaning against the back of her couch, arms outstretched, shirtless.

She gaped. "What do you think you're doing?"

"You used my shirt as a Kleenex. I assumed you did that as a hint I should take it off."

"That is not why I did it."

"So you admit to doing on purpose?"

Clamping her lips, she glared at him.

He couldn't help but laugh. "Come on, baby. Relax. Come have a seat beside me. I promise to only bite the spots that turn you on."

No mistaking the sudden inhalation of breath or the way he could practically feel the heat flushing her skin.

Nice to see she remembers…

"I think it's time you left. Luke's in bed now, so

there's no reason for you to stay."

"And I say there are too many to list. We need to talk, Renny."

"Talk about what? Luke? I told you that you could see him. He knows you're his father. What else do you want from me?"

"You." The single word slipped from him, and he might as well have slapped her given how she recoiled.

"I can't do this, Caleb. Not again."

The utter pain in those words hurt worse than the scars on his body. He also couldn't leave them hovering in the air between them unchallenged. In a flash, he was standing before her.

"Baby." The soft word left his lips as his arms went around her. She held herself stiffly in his embrace at first. Then sighed.

"I promised myself I'd resist you," she murmured.

He brushed his knuckles against the silky skin of her cheek. "I made the same promise to myself."

She lifted her gaze to him. "You suck at keeping promises."

He knew she meant it in jest, but it made him angry. Not angry at her for speaking the truth, but at himself. "I never meant to leave you."

"Then why did you go? Why, Caleb?"

She asked him for an answer, and he wanted to tell her, wanted so desperately for her to understand it wasn't her—it was him. More specifically the monster inside. The cold-blooded beast he couldn't always control.

Since he couldn't find words, none that would

express what he felt, he let instinct guide him. Problem was the survival instinct didn't lead him out the door like he would have expected, but had him dipping his head for a kiss.

She turned her head away, so his lips missed hers but hit the soft skin of her cheek. Undaunted, especially since she didn't move away from his embrace, he let his mouth trail to her ear. She always did love it when he nibbled the lobe.

That hadn't changed. So much hadn't, such as how she made him feel...

A soft sigh escaped her as he tugged at her flesh. Her body softened, and she stepped closer to him, closing the small gap between them.

Coming home. The whispered thought echoed along with a sense of rightness.

Renny fit so perfectly in his arms, her lush body a complement to his hardness. The scent of her, the essence that never failed to enflame the fire simmering within. A fire that burned only for her.

With her melting response to his touch, her body pliant and lush in his arms, he moved his mouth back to hers, and this time, she didn't turn away. Rather, she met him in a sensual embrace, a slow exploration that ignited every single one of his senses. Touch—so silky. Sound—a breathless inhalation. Her taste—more potent than ambrosia. How his entire spirit and soul rejoiced at the joining.

Mine.

And he didn't mean in the owning sense but in the conviction that Renny was the only woman who could ever complete him body, mind, and soul.

The knowledge that she held so much power

over him should have made him tremble. He'd been prisoner to a woman before and suffered, but Renny's control wasn't forced. She didn't compel him to act. It wasn't her fault that her mere presence seduced him and had him forgetting all his promises.

How could he even think to stop when he recollected, all too easily, the fiery nature of her passion? Anticipation kept him from pulling away. Desire had him craving more.

Somehow, he ended up sitting on the couch with her draped in his lap. A good thing, too, since a weakness pervaded his limbs, a fine trembling that permeated every fiber of his being as past and present collided in that moment, striking hard at not only his body, but also his heart.

How could I have ever left her?

Why had it taken him so long to find his way back?

He wrapped his fingers in the silken skein of her hair where it tumbled about her shoulders, pulling her head back that he might trace the fine line of her throat with his lips.

The rapid flutter of her pulse teased him, taunted the beast that wanted to bite, but he pushed back against this urge. He didn't want to hurt Renny. In this, the man part of him would have its way.

The tip of his tongue traced patterns on her skin. His lips tugged soon after. However, he wasn't content with just nibbling at her throat.

I have an urge for something juicier.

Ripe peaches were there for the cupping, and he did, palming the full weight of her breast in his hand while thumbing over the peak. Even through the fabric of her shirt and bra, her nipple reacted, tightening into a bud that protruded. A shudder went through her, and a quick peek at her face meant he caught her licking her lips. He rubbed his thumb lightly over a tip.

Another shiver struck her body, and a soft sigh slipped from her lips.

Enticing didn't come close to describing her.

How could he resist?

Caleb dipped his head and teased the tip of her breast, closing his mouth over it and sucking, the fabric dampening as her breath shortened.

"Caleb." She moaned his name.

My name.

She knew it was him making love to her. Accepted and craved his touch. Emboldened by this knowledge, he pushed at the hem of her shirt, lifting it over the swell of her breasts and revealing her ripe peaches cupped in a plain white bra. She didn't need lace or wires to present her breasts. They were perfect.

Fuller than before, he discovered when he unsnapped the clasp at the back, and yet still high, rounded, and…

"Your nipples are darker." He made the observation aloud and could have kicked himself when she went to cover herself with her hands as if shy or embarrassed.

"That happened during the pregnancy."

The reminder made his lips tighten, and he almost pulled away at the reminder he'd failed. But he held back.

If he left now, would she wonder if it was because he'd said something about her body? He never wanted Renny to feel anything less than perfect, and right now, given she bit her lower lip and still covered herself, he could see she wondered if he still found her attractive.

If you only knew how gorgeous I find you, baby, and how many times you saved me from falling forever into darkness.

He pried her hands away so he could stare at those delicious tits—and they were yummy, enough that his mouth watered. He glanced at her and made sure to catch her gaze. "You're beautiful."

She made a noise. "You're just saying that. I know that I'm heavier than I used to be, and I've got stretch marks."

The extra curve to her frame looked better than fine to him. A man liked a little cushion for the pushing. As to the marks she bore... "You have stretch marks, and I have scars. What of it?" He shrugged. "Life sucks. Shit happens. Sometimes it leaves behind a signature to remind you." Like the fire had left its mark, and yet, in the flames, he'd reclaimed his freedom, so it was a reminder he didn't mind. "Some scars you wear as badges of honor." Such as the marks that meant she'd given birth to life. *My son.* How could she think he would dislike the signs left behind? He traced the skin on her belly, the light silvery trails not bothering him one bit.

She ran her hand down his marred cheek, and he shivered as she touched the never fully healed skin. "You've changed."

Yes. And no. Since he'd left the military, he didn't let his other side out. He no longer *changed*. "I won't deny I went through some stuff that affected me, and yet, in some ways, I remain the same. I never stopped caring for you."

"I don't want to talk about that." Her gaze dropped, and a slight tension tightened her frame.

Smooth move, idiot. You ruined the moment.

Caleb expected her to move away, but she surprised him by leaning forward and capturing his mouth, slanting her lips across his and fiercely kissing him, her teeth clashing against his in her frenzy.

If she preferred to act instead of talk, he was good with that. He was starved for her touch, and given how she undulated against him, he wasn't the only one. She lay back against the couch, and he partially covered her, his body on its side that he might still let his hands roam.

Her Capri-style yoga pants were form-fitting, perfect for a hand that wanted to cup her mound. The heat of her scorched through the fabric, and the moisture of her arousal dampened as well.

Her hips rolled as he pressed the heel of his hand against her, and her breath came in pants. While he rubbed, his lips kept busy pulling and nipping at the nipples that he'd exposed.

Her fingers dug into his scalp, holding him to her breast, her soft mewls of encouragement driving him on.

The heat of her flesh taunted him through her pants. He needed to touch her. Now.

He slid his hand under the waistband and then under the elastic band of her panties. He slid his fingers through downy curls and heard her suck in a breath.

Farther he explored, the tip of his finger touching the damp edge of her nether lips. He parted them before inserting a digit.

Hot. Wet. Tight.

Oh fuck.

He pushed his finger into her, wishing it was his throbbing cock instead, but he didn't want to rush things. Didn't want to ruin this moment.

His mission—give her pleasure. He wanted to hear her cry his name. To feel her climax on his fingers or, even more deliciously, on his tongue.

He inserted a second finger in her, stretching her channel, and as he pumped her sex, he bit down on her nipple while she chanted, "Yes. Yes. Yes."

Her body tensed as she approached the edge. Faster. Faster.

"Yes! Yes!"

The blood-curdling scream didn't come from Renny.

Chapter Ten

"Mommy!" The sharp, shrill scream shattered the moment more effectively than a bucket of cold water.

"Luke!" she cried his name, even as she leaped from the couch. Renny hurriedly tugged down her shirt as she scrambled around the furniture to get to the bedroom.

Caleb took a shortcut, vaulting over the couch and entering the bedroom before she even made it to the door.

Entering, she saw Luke huddled against the headboard while Caleb stood, his entire body bristling, before the window.

The open window.

A cool breeze with hints of bayou filled the room, fluttering the superhero drapes she'd fabricated out of discarded sheets. The moist swamp was a familiar smell, but underlying it was something else, a more pungent scent she couldn't figure out.

"What is that smell?" she asked as she crossed the room and held out her arms to her son. Luke dove into them, seeking their safety.

Remaining staring at the window, Caleb answered her. "I don't know what that is. It's a mixture of a few things, none that make any sense."

Well, that was vague. "Did you leave the

window open when you tucked him in?"

Judging by the tight set of his shoulders and the shake of his head, no. Despite the ambient temperature, a shiver went through her.

Who opened the window? And more disturbing, why?

"I saw something," Luke sobbed, fear making him a little boy again who clung to his mother.

"What did you see, bug?" She bounced him in her arms, a familiar motion begun when he was just little and needed soothing from a tummy ache or a new tooth.

"The dinosaur found me. It wants to eat me!"

"It was just a bad dream, bug. Dinosaurs don't exist."

The right words for a situation like this, and yet she couldn't deny something had happened. Someone or something had opened that window and left behind a smell that unpleasantly lingered.

Caleb stuck his head and part of his upper body out the window, which she realized, on top of being open, was missing its screen. Could Luke sense the fear in her because he clung tighter, his body seized in terror? He obviously believed something had tried to get in and, more worrisome, given Caleb's actions, he did too.

Who, though, would come after her son?

The same thing that scared the twins and did something to Melanie. Was something dangerous hiding in the bayou? It wouldn't be the first time.

"What's going on, Caleb?" she asked in a voice that sounded too high-pitched, but she couldn't help it. She held her son's head cradled to her as she bounced him on her hip.

Turning from the window, Caleb met her gaze. His big shoulders rolled in a shrug. "I don't know what the hell is going on, but I don't like it. Something tried to get in here."

At his words, Luke whimpered and buried his head deeper into her shoulder.

A growl rumbled, and Renny couldn't help but take a step back as Caleb's eyes glinted feral green, his inner beast rising for a moment.

She couldn't help but be frightened—and fascinated. While she knew Caleb was a shifter, she'd never actually gotten to see his other side, almost as if he was ashamed of it.

Or frightened.

Others had no problem letting their beast out to stretch. It wasn't unusual to see them sometimes roaming at night, although Daryl's black panther was hard to truly see.

However, Caleb didn't revel in his otherness like others did. He kept it tucked away, except during times of intense emotion. Then, and only then, did he sometimes slip enough for the croc to rise.

A brief glimpse was all she got before Caleb slammed the door closed and his eyes turned normal again, but his body still bristled.

"You can't stay here." Flatly said.

She didn't disagree, but there was one problem with his assessment. "I have nowhere else to go." Not entirely true. She could probably crash at Melanie's place, but given the twins' fright that afternoon, did she dare dump her own troubles and fear on them?

Determination straightened Caleb's spine, and

his eyes glinted, almost as if he prepared for battle.

Which means I probably won't like his suggestion.

"You have somewhere to go where I can keep you safe. My place."

He was right. She didn't like it at all.

But when it came to the safety of her son, she didn't have a choice.

Chapter Eleven

It surprised Caleb that Renny didn't protest much when he told her she was coming with him back to his place. More actually his mother's home, but he didn't think Ma would protest, not when he knew she was dying to meet her grandson.

"Give me a minute to grab some things," was what she murmured instead. Even more amazing, when he held out his arms to take his son, Luke dove at him, arms and legs winding as far as they could go around his body.

It took Renny but a few minutes to pack a bag while Luke lay nestled against Caleb's chest, the trust his son had in him almost enough to bring a grown man to tears.

A quick scratch of his groin took care of that urge.

Loving his family was all well and good, but he couldn't let debilitating emotions cloud his senses. *I need to be alert and ready because danger lurks.*

Something threatened his family, and he had to protect them.

Funny how in less than one day, he'd gone from wondering if he'd ever fit in, from promising to stay away from Renny, to almost sleeping with her, instantly bonding with his son, and now pledging to take care of them both.

Guess I'm sticking around.

And he'd kill anyone who tried to make him leave again.

Bite them good.

Slam that door shut. He didn't need help from that part of himself.

When it came time to leave the apartment, Caleb had to hand Luke to his mother since he wanted his hands free just in case whatever tried to come in had lingered. However, his son refused to be carried.

"I'm not a baby," Luke announced with a jut of his lower lip.

"Of course you're not," Caleb said when he saw the hurt look on Renny's face. "But do me a favor, would you, big guy? Can you hold onto your mother's hand? She looks kind of scared. It's your job to keep her safe until we get to the car."

Slim chest swelling in pride, in pajamas sporting—groan—smiling alligators, Luke gripped his mother's hand.

With Caleb leading the way, emerging on the outside landing and checking for signs of danger, they descended the steps to the sidewalk and quickly moved to the car.

Nothing marred the serenity of the evening. Not even a breeze. And forget the hum of crickets.

There was nothing but the noise they made as their feet hit the sidewalk.

Caleb didn't trust the quiet one bit. "Get in the car," he ordered.

As Renny opened the rear passenger door, Caleb scanned the shadows. There were too many, and forget sifting scents. Whatever tried to climb through the window had left a lingering stench that permeated the air in all directions.

What the fuck is it?

The answer tickled on the edge of his senses, a part of him taunting him with the feeling of familiarity, but at the same time, there was an alien quality to the scent, a sensation of wrongness that made his skin prickle and the croc in his head snap its teeth.

Bite the enemy.

Stop with all the biting. Behave.

The last thing Caleb needed was to lose control of his beast in front of Luke and Renny. He would frighten them for sure. But even worse, what if he couldn't control the reptile he shared a body with? What if *it* happened again?

Once he'd seen Renny and Luke safely into their seats, Caleb made his way to the driver's spot that Renny had left for him.

Sliding behind the wheel, he stared at the push button lock on the door. "You don't even have automatic locks?"

With a spark in her eyes, Renny slammed her hand down on her lock and was immediately copied by Luke. "Is that auto enough for you?"

Yeah, things would have to change around here, starting with the standard of living. Damned if Caleb was going to have his child growing up wanting for shit like he had.

Don't mistake him. His mom had done her best, but one working parent of two busy boys—who went through pants and shoes like no one's business—meant her paychecks had to stretch, and they went without a lot.

But not my kid.

His kid would have the best of everything, even if he had to swallow his pride to get a job. A job, he'd worry about that in the morning. First, he had to get everyone to safety.

The drive to his mom's place was done in silence, the radio in her car not managing more than the occasional spurts of music in between static. He didn't have the breath to sigh anymore when she offered an apologetic, "Antenna snapped off."

It didn't take long to get to his place, but it was long enough for one tired little guy to almost fall asleep.

Renny didn't protest when Caleb was the one to scoop their son from the backseat and carry him into the house.

Oddly, Princess, the rabid squirrel that seemed to think the house was her fortress, didn't erupt into a cacophony of barking. First time since he'd arrived, and Caleb was thankful for it. He swore the dog took sadistic pleasure in lying in wait just out of sight so she could dart at him with sharp barks and a flash of teeth meant to suck a man's balls into his stomach.

A quick glance to his left, across the kitchen, showed his mother's bedroom door was closed and no light showed in the seams. Years of early work shifts meant Ma went to bed by nine p.m. However, Constantine was still up, his furry rat nestled in his lap, one beady eyed trained on Caleb. She didn't bark, but Caleb saw the glint in her gaze and the lift of her lip that said, *I'm watching you.*

His brother raised a brow in his direction, probably wondering at the sleepy child Caleb held and the fact that Renny entered at his heels.

It only took a silent shake of Caleb's head to stem the questions he could see brimming in Constantine's eyes.

As Caleb went down the hall to his room, he only paused a moment to point out the open door that led into the bathroom. Given the secretive nature of his relationship with Renny before, they'd never really hung out at his place. They'd spent most of their moments in the bayou, the soft moss their fragrant bower, the cloud-dappled sky their cover.

Entering his room, which had remained surprisingly untouched during his absence, Caleb pulled back the neatly tucked cover—some military training didn't fade so easily—and lay Luke on the sheet.

Renny came alongside him and pulled up the thick blanket before placing a soft kiss on Luke's forehead, but when she would have left, Luke made a sound.

"Don't be scared, bug, Mommy's not going anywhere." Without a glance or word at Caleb, Renny slid into the other side of the bed and snuggled their child close.

Was it weird to want to climb in, too?

He would have liked to wrap his arms around them both and reassure them he would keep them safe.

I won't let you down again.

Perhaps she sensed this newest vow, a vow he could keep to his death. Whatever the reason, when Renny peeked at him, he was glad of the silence because he wasn't sure he could have spoken in that moment. In her eyes he saw trust.

After all I did…she trusts me to protect them.

Before he could embarrass himself and beg to climb in bed with them—and probably collapse the damned frame—Caleb left, shutting the door softly behind him.

For a moment, he stood in the hall, head bowed, simply trying to breathe. The panic, held at bay the entire time, rushed over him in a wave. Sucking in gasping breaths, he sank to his haunches, dizzy, while his legs lacked the strength to hold him.

How can I keep them safe?

He couldn't even keep himself safe.

I can't let them down.

Not again.

Never again.

So man the fuck up!

Stop the fucking pity party and take charge. He wasn't a coward. He wasn't a weakling.

Taking deep breaths, he pushed the panic back. He forced strength into his limbs and stood. He took the steps needed to get away from the door that separated him from the two most important things in his world and practically staggered into the living room.

"I need a beer." But he wouldn't have one. Not when he needed his senses clear.

"I would have said more like a head check," Constantine remarked from his spot on the couch. "Is it me, or did you just bring a kid and his mother over for a sleepover?"

"I did." A sleepover he wasn't quite invited to.

"I'm a little confused, though. How are you supposed to bang Renny with a kid around?"

Caleb wasn't even aware he'd moved, and he also didn't care just how big his little brother was. He hauled him by the shirt off the couch and snarled, "Don't you fucking disrespect her."

"I think I've got a long ways to go before I catch up to your act, *big brother*," Constantine said with a sneer. "Do you even know the meaning of respect?"

"I know enough to tell you that I won't have you bad-mouthing Renny."

"Don't worry. I wasn't planning to say shit about her. But you on the other hand...I will mock you anytime I like. Especially when I have a problem with your screwing up Renny and the boy's life again."

"Who says I'm going to screw them?"

"You did once before. I hear it's easier the second time."

Easier? Was Constantine nuts? "Nothing about leaving here and her was ever easy. I regretted it every fucking day."

"And yet you still went. Stayed away for years, not giving a damn about anyone else. Now you come back and you say these pretty words about staying and making up for shit. Can you blame me if I don't believe you?"

"No. I guess you'll have to give me time to prove myself."

"Problem with time is you get a chance to hurt Renny and her boy again."

"What I do with them is none of your business."

"I disagree. This is my house, and I've got a right to know what the hell is going on. That is my nephew down that hall." Constantine stabbed a finger in that direction. "And I'll be damned if I'm going to sit back and let you fuck with him. He doesn't deserve that, and neither does she."

"First of all, how many fucking times do I have to say I'm sorry?" It wasn't easy keeping his voice low and under control, but Caleb tried. The walls of his house weren't thick, and while the air conditioners in the windows provided a quelling hum, he didn't need Renny and his son being disturbed by his still prickly relationship with his brother. "I fucked up. Okay? I fucked up large, and I know it's going to take a lot of apologizing and shit to make people forgive me for it. But I'm trying, dammit."

"By dragging Renny and her boy out in the middle of the night?" his brother asked with incredulity.

"You would have done the same. Twice now, something's come after my son." Caleb quickly brought his brother up to speed. By the time he'd told him about the incident at the picnic, the grocery store, and the latest mishap at Renny's place, Constantine had a pensive look.

"It's happening again."

Well, that wasn't what Caleb expected to hear. "What's happening again? What the hell are you talking about?"

Constantine met his gaze. "I keep forgetting you didn't keep up with the local news. Or at least the shifter news from our town. It first started a few years back."

"Hold on to that train of thought." Caleb held up a hand. "Don't tell me yet. Let's go outside and you can explain what you mean while I check the perimeter of the property."

Because while they'd driven several miles out of

town, that thing, whatever it was stalking his child, had obviously no problem traveling or tracking.

Outside the house, the hum of the window cooling units was louder, but despite that, Caleb could hear the comforting sound of crickets and other bayou noises. Nothing out of the ordinary approached, but still, it never hurt to be sure.

As Caleb set off to walk around the house, eyes on the ground watching for prints, Constantine launched into a recap of some of the weird shit plaguing Bitten Point.

"So about two years or so after you left, we had a rash of disappearances. No men, just a few women and children. All shifters."

"Abductions or murders?"

His brother shrugged. "We never really did find out. A few of those who went missing turned back up with no memory of what had happened while others…" He trailed off.

"Never came back?"

"Nope. They vanished as if into thin air."

Or as if swallowed by the bayou. The swamps knew how to keep a secret—and a body.

"How long did this go on for?"

"Not too long. Two-three weeks at most. But at the time it was happening, there was talk among some of the children that they'd seen a monster."

"That looked like a dinosaur?" Caleb asked.

"Actually, no, the rumors I heard said it was a wolfman, all fur and big teeth and claws."

"A Lycan, in the bayou?" An incredulous note entered Caleb's voice.

"No, as in a wolfman that walked on two legs,

which we know is impossible."

"Not really." Caleb's discoveries outside the bayou shattered many long-held beliefs.

"What do you mean not really?"

"It means that some of the things we grew up thinking were absolute aren't. Shifters can walk on two legs, or four, or even eight." Shudder. That one still gave him nightmares. "While the ability to shapeshift into a hybrid form is rare, it does exist. I've seen it."

For a moment, his brother simply blinked at him. "Well, hot damn. Can you do it?"

He couldn't lie. "Yes, but I don't recommend it." The mix of man and croc at once made for a strange mental process, but it was better than leaving the croc in utter control.

"Don't recommend it? But why?" His brother's face lit up. "I could be snakeman!"

For a moment, the Goliath that was his brother reminded him of the little boy Caleb used to have following him around, hero worship in his eyes.

"Snakeman?" Caleb couldn't help a teasing lilt. "Leaving a slimy trail everywhere he slithers."

While Caleb took after their dead father and became a crocodile, Constantine, took after their mother, a python. Given his bulk now, Caleb had to wonder just how big his snake had gotten. He wasn't sure if he wanted to find out.

"Snakes don't leave gooey trails." Constantine drew himself straight and adopted a haughty sneer. "Try more like crushing his enemy in his mighty grip."

"Hugging is not a fighting technique."

"Neither are nibbles, crockie."

"I've been trained to fight."

"I guess they threw in the asshole lessons for free."

The rebuke was tossed without any real malice, making it even more effective. "Sorry."

"Whatever. I think from now on, instead of saying sorry, we should start a jar. Twenty bucks every time you say it. I figure within a week, I'll be able to afford a whole new set of tires for my truck."

The fist slugged his brother's arm before Caleb could think twice. It was a habit from his military days when he and the boys shot the shit. For a moment, he could only gape at his brother, wondering how Constantine would take it.

He grinned. "Didn't hurt."

At those familiar words, Caleb did laugh. How many times had they used that phrase growing up, trying to prove who was toughest?

As far as he recalled, Caleb had been in the lead from the time he got shot with buckshot in the ass and grinned—over gritted teeth—while Ma yanked the pellets out with tweezers.

As their laughter died down, Caleb heard a rustle to his left. He zeroed his gaze in, staring at the shadows bordering the yard, the dense foliage providing so many possible hiding spots.

If his years in the military had taught Caleb anything, it was to never underestimate the enemy. Where there was a will, there was a way, and he still had trouble even months after leaving the war overseas in looking at the world with a less than jaundiced eye.

What of the heavy boughs weighed down by lush leaves? Ambush could await the unwary in the treetops. Anyone or thing could lie under the mud and weeds, ready to rise. The enemy could be inside his own mind, waiting to burst free from its bodily prison and rampage.

Let me out. I can scout.

Indeed, his reptile half could, but would the cold creature stop at just that? And what really could his croc self do that the man couldn't?

I know danger is lurking. It can be anywhere.

Knowing this, Caleb would stand on guard, as a man, to stop it.

Since nothing seemed to be disturbing the nightlife—the bayou sounds rolled over his skin—Caleb questioned his brother further about this supposed wolfman haunting the bayou years ago. "I take it they never caught the guy, or wolf, or whatever that was abducting folks?"

Constantine shook his head. "Nope. One day, a kid riding his bike got snatched, the next he was found sitting in the park, no idea how he got there. And that was the last time it happened. Until now."

"So today marks the first incidents?"

"Maybe."

"What do you mean, maybe?" Caleb narrowed his gaze at his brother.

"We got a call into the station"—the fire station where Constantine worked as a firefighter—"that something might have taken up residence in the pond by the park. A bunch of kids claimed they saw something, and since we didn't want any of them getting eaten in case a croc or gator did make its way there, we took a truck out and met up with some of the boys in blue. We dragged the pond and came up empty."

"But?" Caleb prodded, fixing his brother with a stare.

"There was this smell. A weird one."

"Kind of reptile like, but not quite, with a hint of something wrong," Caleb said.

"I would have said more like alien, but yeah. And as for tracks, nothing that made sense."

"What do you mean?"

"I mean did you ever see something that walked with one human foot and one clawed and webbed one?"

No, Caleb hadn't, which was why he slept on the couch that night with a gun under his pillow, one eye open, and an ear cocked to see if the pop-can trap he'd strung outside all the windows rattled.

But the best intentions didn't keep the nightmares at bay.

The flames slithered closer, dancing bright devils eager to taste anything they could lick. Caleb tugged at his tethers. However, the rope bound him tight.

A prisoner waiting for punishment because he'd dared disobey.

Begging wasn't an option.

Not only would he never stoop so low, there was no one left to hear his pleas.

And still the torrid fire burned closer.

Let me out.

His beast pulsed, demanding exit.

Again, he pulled at the thick twine crisscrossing his wrists. He'd managed to somewhat fray them against the rough stone surface of the wall, but not enough to snap himself free.

There is no choice. Let me out.

The heat pulsed against his skin, crisping his hairs, tightening pores already dry. He didn't want to let the beast out. He could hear the screams of battle. Scent the blood...

Yummy.

The thought repulsed him. The thought made him hunger.

It wasn't right. He shouldn't revel in the wild nature of his croc. Shouldn't crave the same things.

I am a man.

You are also a predator.

He was also on fire. The flames licked at his skin, attracted to the scraps of clothes he still wore, singeing the rope holding him prisoner. But he didn't have time to wait for the flames to free him, not when his skin bubbled.

He screamed, not with pain, but out of frustration. How ironic that the reason he found himself tied was what would save him. He wouldn't unleash his beast for the enemy, but he would have to in order to survive.

His croc snapped in glee.

The change came on fast and vicious, his skin hardening into scales, the shape of his face, his hands, his whole body contorting, reshaping, becoming...a crocodile.

Not a friendly one. Nor a small one.

Last time they measured him, he was over twelve feet from snout to tail. How he managed to expand to that size, he never could figure out. He did know that he and others of his kind took heavier than

131

he looked to a whole new level.

Unleashing his beast didn't stop the flames from kissing his skin. Flesh sizzled.

Smells good.

He would have gagged if he wasn't just a passenger on the reptile train bent on escape—and destruction.

In a frenzy from being cooped away, in pain, and pissed when someone dared shoot at him, Caleb could do nothing to stop his vicious side from lunging at the guy with the gun.

The crunch of bone, the coppery taste of blood, the exultation, his personal horror that he enjoyed it.

No.

No!

Hands touched him. Soft hands. Along with a faint murmur.

"It's all right, Caleb. It's just a dream. Wake up."

Renny! In a flash, his eyes opened, and he saw Renny leaning over him, too close, too tempting.

Let's taste.

Since he didn't know if it was man or beast talking, he barked, "Stay away from me."

She recoiled, as if slapped. "Well, excuse me for waking you up."

He rubbed a hand over his face. "I'm sorry. I don't always react well when woken." He'd punched bigger men than her for daring to lay a hand on him when resting.

"Good to know. Next time you have a nightmare, I'll throw things at you from afar."

Next time?

She seemed to realize her faux pas at the same

time he did. He couldn't help a smile. "Does this mean you're sticking around?"

"I think that's a better question to ask you," she retorted.

It came to his notice it was pitch-black outside, and a quick peek over at the DVD player showed a neon-lit time of three twenty-three a.m. "Why are you up? Did you hear something?" He swung his legs so he sat on the couch.

Blonde hair flew as Renny shook her head. "I had to use the bathroom and, on the way back, heard you mumbling in your sleep. Do you have nightmares often?"

A lie would preserve his dignity. He went with the truth. "Every night unless I take the pills the doctor gave me."

"You didn't take them before bed?"

"Of course not. I can't protect you if I'm passed out cold."

"Oh, Caleb." She breathed his name and took a step toward him, a moving shadow that didn't rouse the panic. Another thing rose in its stead. "Are the nightmares from the fire?"

"Yes and no. The fire is almost always part of it." Yet it was the chaos after, where he fought to escape, that plagued his dreams the most.

Renny seated herself gingerly on the couch beside him. "I'm sorry."

He couldn't help a rusty laugh. "You're sorry? You are the person who needs to least apologize."

"Then what do you want me to feel? Pity? I doubt you'd appreciate that."

"There's only one thing I want from you."

Her eyes met his in the darkness, and he could read the longing in their gaze, but also the fear. "And that's the one thing I don't know if I can ever give."

With those words, Renny fled. A good thing, too, else he might have taken his croc's advice.

Claim her. Because there was one thing becoming crystal clear. He needed Renny in his life. But if he moved too quickly, she might run. And he couldn't lose her again.

Chapter Twelve

Run. Run.

Renny's chest heaved as she struggled for breath running through the bayou, the thick air cloying in her lungs. Mud squelched between her bare toes, the suctioning pull slowing her pace while rapier weeds whipped at her bared legs. Her nightgown ended mid-thigh and provided no protection.

Just like the moon taunted her, refusing to hide in shadow and help her blend into the darkness.

Splash.

The sudden spray of water as her foot slammed into a puddle drew a short cry from her. Way to pinpoint her location even more. She paused for a moment, unable to hide her ragged pants for air.

Nothing marred the silence but her harsh breathing. Not a sound.

But she knew it was there. Hunting. Chasing. Hungering…

Frantically, Renny cast about looking for a spot to hide. Anywhere.

The swaying fronds and the glitter of water mocked her until she looked to her left. There, not so far from her, was a hill.

It wouldn't hide her from the monster that wanted her, but the man sitting atop the knoll would protect her.

He cast his gaze down and caught hers. A vivid green flare flashed in his eyes.

Caleb.

Caleb was here. He would keep her safe.

Energized, she ran toward him, and he saw her coming. She knew he did. But the beast came as well.

Who would arrive first?

Arms outstretched, she reached for him, even as the fetid breath of the monster washed over her back.

"Caleb! Help me. Caleb." She said his name on a plea.

Surely he heard her, and yet he turned away.

And the jaws of the beast—

With a choked cry, Renny sat upright in bed, her skin clammy, her heart racing—and remarkably uneaten.

Thank God. I'm alive.

But alone.

Oh no! Where was Luke?

Casting back the covers, Renny searched under them in case they hid Luke's small body, but he wasn't there, nor was he anywhere in the room.

Braless, but at least decently clothed in a T-shirt and her yoga pants—because she'd not had the energy to change into something else, not with all that happened—Renny felt no qualms about exiting the room to hunt down her son. She made it to the end of the hall before she halted.

Frozen, she barely dared breathe as she watched—and tried not to cry.

Still wearing his pajamas, Luke stood on the edge of the kitchen watching as Claire bustled around making a pot of coffee, softly humming.

"Are you my grandma?"

The scream Claire let out could have woken the dead. She whirled, one hand clutching her chest, her wide eyes staring at Luke, who tilted his head quizzically.

"Sweet mother of God. How did you get here?"

"Daddy brought me on account of the dinosaur."

To her credit, Claire didn't react to the interesting excuse as to his presence. "Yes, those dinos can be annoying. Why don't you have a seat, and I'll make you some breakfast. Would you like some pancakes?"

"Yes please, Grandma."

Claire turned around to putter in the cabinets and fire on the stove, but not before Renny caught the glimmer of tears, tears that also filled her own eyes.

What have I done?

When she'd realized Caleb didn't want her or their child, Renny had floundered. She hadn't grown up with an extended family. Her dad, an ornery bear in real life, cut all ties with his family out west when he moved to Florida to be with Renny's mother, a human and an orphan. As a result, Renny didn't grow up with grandparents.

When Renny found out about her pregnancy, her first inclination was to make sure Caleb knew first. Except Caleb never replied, and given he didn't show an interest, she hesitated telling Caleb's mom out of fear she'd get the same reaction that she'd gotten from her father.

"Whore. Spreading your legs for that no account reptile. Your mother would be so ashamed."

Indeed, Mother would have hung her head, just not for the reason her father thought. Poor Daddy had changed so much.

Still, though, her father's words gave her pause. In her naïve logic, she assumed since Caleb knew about her pregnancy, he would tell his mother. What she'd not counted on was Caleb never finding out, which meant Claire never knew she had a grandson.

Four years lost because of foolish choices.

Say it like it is. Pride kept you from saying anything.

It didn't feel good to realize that she'd made a major error. Renny had been so mad at Caleb, so mad at the injustice of the world in general, that she had ended up hurting someone who would have dearly loved her son.

But I have a chance to start making things right.

And if she could make amends, didn't that mean Caleb had that right, too?

Speak of the devil... She felt him before she heard him. "I thought I heard a scream."

"Our son introduced himself to your mother."

Caleb sniffed. "Judging by the smell of bacon and pancakes, they're getting along."

His light tone did not assuage the heaviness crushing her chest. "I'm so sorry, Caleb. I feel utterly wretched about not bringing Luke over to meet your mom. I never meant to hurt anyone."

"I know how that works, baby. Best we can do is move forward and try to not repeat our mistakes."

Turning, she took in not only his serious mien but also his clean-shaven jaw, button-up shirt, and slick, wet hair. Utterly handsome and obviously planning an outing. "Going somewhere?"

"Well, it is Sunday." At her rounded O of surprise, he laughed. "Before you think I've turned to religion, I've got a job interview."

"You do?" She blinked in surprise. This was the first she'd heard of it.

"Yeah, I do. I'm already getting a check from the military, apparently my service and scars are worth something to them, but it's not going to be enough for us to get a decent place."

"Get us a what?" She took a step back from him, trying to decipher his words. "Are you talking about us moving in together?"

"After last night—"

She held up a hand to stop him. "What happened last night was…"

"Special."

"I was going to say rash. You just got back in to town, and I feel like things are moving too fast."

"Then I'll slow down."

"What if I want you to stop?" She didn't, but at the same time, Renny felt as if she wasn't thinking clearly. Caleb touched her, and she just melted. She forgot all the reasons for keeping him at arm's length.

He bowed his head, a big man humbled and defeated in front of her. "If that's what you truly want."

No. She didn't want him to go away. She wanted more of his kisses and hugs and…him. But could she handle the heartbreak if Caleb betrayed her again? "I can't be with you. Not like that." Even if just saying it made her feel as if her heart was shattering into a thousand pieces.

His shoulders slumped as her words hit him. But only for a moment. "Too bad because I'm not giving up." His head snapped up, and his eyes blazed, one hundred percent human, but determined. "I lost you once because I didn't fight hard enough, and I'll be damned if I lose you again. This might not be what you want to hear, baby, but the fact of the matter is, I'm here to stay. I will be a father to my son, and"—he lowered his voice—"we will share a bed." Even if he had to handcuff himself at night so he could sleep beside her without worry.

"Caleb—"

He didn't give her a chance to finish her reply, simply slanted his mouth over hers in a hard kiss that lasted but a second. Then he was walking past her and out into the kitchen, where he ruffled Luke's hair, gave his mother a loud smooch on the cheek, and stole a piece of bacon all before heading out the door with a casually tossed, "I'll be back in a few hours. Don't leave the house until I return."

Of course she couldn't leave, she thought with bemusement. He'd taken her car to go to his interview, leaving her to face the consequences of her actions. Alone.

Face your actions.

Taking a deep breath, she walked into the kitchen with a, "Good morning, Claire."

Renny couldn't deny she deserved the hard look Caleb's mother shot her. "Renny. Why don't you park yourself on a stool while I wrangle some breakfast on a plate for you? Then, I want to hear everything about my grandson."

It took a while to tell Claire everything. Some parts were harder than others. It involved a few tears, which Claire shared with her, a comrade spirit when it came to raising a child on her own. By the time it was done—an eye-rolling Constantine having stolen Luke long before so he wouldn't start craving dolls and a tea set—Renny knew, no matter what happened with Caleb, she wasn't alone.

"You and Luke are family," which, as Claire explained with a wave in the direction of the sink, meant Renny got to do the dishes. Blech.

Chapter Thirteen

Beggars can't be choosers.

That mantra did little to ease Caleb's irritation when he realized the interview he'd set up the previous night by email was going to be with Wes Mercer, who predictably smirked when Caleb arrived at the Bittech building for his ten a.m. appointment.

"Well, look at what dragged itself into my office." If by office, a windowless room loaded with monitors counted.

Pride made Caleb want to spin on his heel and say fuck it. Pride also made him stay because he had people depending on him. "I like this about as much as you do, which means not fucking much."

"Pretty stupid thing to say considering you're here looking for a job." Wes leaned back in his seat and steepled his fingers, a smirk on his lips.

Caleb set his jaw and held his fists tight at his sides, resisting the temptation to wipe the smirk off Wes's face. "Not stupid, honest. I'm not going to pretend I suddenly like you. Nor am I going to shove my nose up your ass for a job."

"Keep going, although I should mention that, so far, you're not really winning me over. As a matter of fact, I'm thinking you should probably just turn right around and *do* let the door smack you on the way out."

"I am royally fucking this up." Caleb sighed.

"Listen, I need this position." He really did. He'd asked around, and unless he was willing to bag groceries, wash dishes, or go bayou fishing, which would put him out of reach if Renny or Luke needed him, then, "This job is the best choice in town."

Bittech didn't just offer a decent wage, as his brother had explained, it provided benefits to an employee and his dependents.

And fuck me. I've got dependents now.

Wes spun away from him and drummed his fingers on the countertop bolted to the wall. The laminate surface formed a ring around the room under the monitors. Atop it sat a half-dozen keyboards and wireless mice. "You do realize that, by coming to work here, you'd be taking orders from me."

Something that still surprised Caleb considering Wes was his age and seemed rather young for the position of head of security.

"I know how to take orders." Too well, as a matter of fact. Except, this time, Caleb would do it by choice, not compulsion.

"What about breaking the rules?" The question emerged oddly, and Caleb noted Wes watching him intently.

"I'm not a rule breaker." His mother had raised him poor, but right.

"What if you had to in order to keep people safe?"

Caleb's brow knit into a frown. "What are you saying?"

"I'm wondering if I can trust you."

"Depends. Trust me to hold your beer while you jump off a cliff, probably. Trust me to not call you a dickhead behind your back, probably not."

Wes snickered. "You know, if you weren't such an asshole, I could almost like you."

"Dude, don't say shit like that. It's creepy."

"What's creepy is the fact I'm even thinking of telling you what's happening."

"Tell me what?"

For a moment, Wes didn't reply. Then he blew out a hard breath. "Fuck it. You haven't been around so you probably don't know and aren't involved."

"Involved in what? Stop acting all mysterious like and spit it out."

"I'm talking about the testing going on here."

Baffled, Caleb blurted out, "What fucking testing?"

"I mean the testing happening right here in the Bittech labs."

"Rewind for a minute so I can understand because I must be missing something. You're saying Bittech is testing folks. Isn't that what a lab is supposed to do?"

"Yes, and on the surface, that's fine. What's not fine is the fact they're not just taking samples from those volunteering. They're bringing in samples from folks who have no idea."

"How can people not know? I mean, I'm pretty sure I'd notice if someone was sticking me with a needle and drawing blood."

"In some cases, they're stealing it from employers, like the fire station, which is mandated to drug test its guys every so often. And the vet, who sends Bittech samples to check for disease and viruses."

Again, not a huge deal, given shifter blood samples could only go to those in on the secret, like Bittech. "So they're keeping samples sent to them. I'm not seeing the big deal yet."

"Because there are other samples they've gotten that weren't freely given. My Uncle Bob, who hasn't seen a doctor since the summer of eighty-seven when he tangled with that nest of vipers, has a file. As does Kerry, my cousin, even though she just moved into town three months ago. There are lots of others, too. Seems like they're documenting everyone in town."

"But why?" Caleb asked.

At that query, Wes shrugged. "Fucked if I know. Initially, the lab was started back in the seventies so that our scientists could study our condition. It then evolved into the doctors helping the hybrid couples get pregnant"—because mixed species didn't procreate easily—"and they've also been working on fabricating our own form of medicine for those rare diseases our shapeshifting genes can't combat. When it comes to cases such as those, I can understand why they kept stuff on file. But the samples I saw numbered in the hundreds. Your brother is in there. Your mother, too. What the hell do they need those samples for?"

A valid question, but it raised others. "How do you know about all this?"

Wes smiled. "As head of security, I see lots of stuff, even things I'm not supposed to. Things that don't make sense, like the number of humans now working here."

"Humans?" Caleb couldn't help an incredulous note. "I could have sworn my brother said most of the people working here are either one of us or in on the secret."

"They used to be. A few months ago, the institute went on a hiring spree. Humans mostly. Humans who don't start out knowing what we are but are told once they pass a few tests. The company has been giving them samples of our blood and hair to play with."

A chill went through Caleb. Hadn't he heard rumors while in the military of scientists messing around with their blood? The whispers at the time were frightening if true. *They're creating an army of monsters.*

And, yes, he meant create. While birth could result in the creation of new shifters, it wasn't always the case. Look at Renny, whose ursine-based father produced an unenhanced daughter.

I don't know that I'd call her unenhanced. Renny might not turn into something with claws, but she was definitely special.

So special that even her father's attempt to have her *changed* didn't take root. See, people could *become* shifters as well. But it wasn't simple. Nothing so easy as a scratch or a bite like the movies portrayed. The creation of a new shifter required the exchange of fluids, lots of fluids, blood being the vehicle of choice, siphoned out of a host and filtered into a human. Not that hard to do with today's technology, but it didn't always work. Most bodies rejected the shifter gene. Some theorized it made sure they didn't overpopulate. Probably a good thing, given the animal within didn't always play nice with others.

"What are the scientists looking for?" Caleb asked.

"That's what I wanted to know, so I asked

Andrew."

"And?"

"The little prick told me to mind my fucking business. That all work conducted was being done with the full knowledge of the High Council, and that if I knew what was good for me, I'd keep my mouth shut."

"The little prick actually threatened you? And you didn't kill him?"

Nothing changed outwardly. Wes still wore his human guise, yet when he smiled, white teeth gleaming, it was all gator. "It was close."

"Andrew doesn't want you blabbing, yet here you are telling me this."

"Sometimes a man needs allies."

"Since when are we on the same team?"

"Since something doesn't smell right, and as much as I dislike you, I don't think you'd stand by and watch this town get fucked."

No, he wouldn't, but he also wasn't sure what his plans were yet. "I just got back into town and already you're trying to drag me into something. I came back for a fresh start, not to get involved in some kind of conspiracy theory. I mean, come on, so far, other than letting humans in on the secret, your evidence is pretty slim. I mean, if the High Council is backing it…" Caleb shrugged.

"That doesn't mean jack shit, and you know it. You don't think it's kind of fishy that here's a medical lab, screwing with shifter DNA, and suddenly we're getting messed-up reports of giant lizards running amok?" Paranoia was a shifter's best friend.

"It could still be a coincidence." Said even if Caleb didn't believe it. "Have you talked to anyone else about it?"

"Like who? Most folks in town are in Bittech's back pocket, and those that aren't ain't interested in rocking the boat."

Didn't that sound familiar? Not so long ago, Caleb had been part of a group that knew something was fishy with their military unit. Everyone seemed to know something hinky was going on, and yet, they did nothing about it. And once they confirmed what was happening, it was too late.

I am not sitting back and watching anymore. I will take control of my destiny and like fuck am I letting anyone use me or the people I know.

"If I'm understanding you correctly, you think they're doing more than research. You think they're experimenting." Making monsters.

Wes shrugged. "Damned if I know. Maybe I am just being a paranoid freak. Maybe they're looking for a cure to the swamp fever. Or some kind of hair growth product for humans that they'll sell for a fortune in the marketplace."

"I still don't get why you're telling me. Of all the people to trust…" Caleb spread his hands. "Excuse me if I'm still a touch skeptical."

The other man leaned forward and fixed him with a gaze, his mien serious. "Be skeptical, but be vigilant. Be informed, because what if I'm right? What if this is the start of something that could hurt us all?"

"Don't tell me you've gone heroic?" The swamp would freeze over the day a Mercer turned into a knight for fairness, morality, and justice.

A moue twisted Wes's lips. "Perish the fucking thought. This decision to figure out what the hell is happening is totally selfish because, if shit hits the fan, then my life might get difficult. I'd rather spend my life doing an easy job, going home to drink beer and banging pretty girls than constantly looking over my shoulder waiting for a silver bullet because someone outed us to the world."

A valid fear they all shared. Since as far back as Caleb could remember, the anxiety of the humans finding out they existed was huge. No one seemed to doubt that the revelation of their secret would result in humans loading up on silver ammo and blood-thirsty outrage.

Yeah, that didn't put a lot of faith in mankind. However, to test the theory, they'd have to admit werewolves and other creatures lived among them. No one was willing to risk possibly starting a genocide.

Which meant that, if Wes was on to something, then Caleb couldn't walk away.

"What do you want me to do?" Caleb asked.

"First off, I want someone other than me to know."

"Worried about getting taken out?"

"I don't plan on rolling belly up in the bayou yet, but it never hurts to have someone else in on the secret. Second, start watching."

"Watching what?"

"Bittech. The town. Anything really. I'm going to hire you so you can move around the institute legitimately. Something weird is going on, something that has my gator senses tingling. We've got to find out what's happening and put a stop to it."

"Sounds easy enough so long as we have the understanding that this does not mean we're friends."

Dark brows drew together as Wes frowned. "Never. Once this is over, we shall return to status quo."

Excellent. Caleb did so have fun screwing with Wes. He'd learned some awesome pranks in the military.

"So are you in?" Wes asked.

"I'm in. *Boss.*" Caleb couldn't hide the smirk as he said it.

"Actually, you will address me as Mr. Mercer." Even bigger smirk volleyed back.

The things Caleb had to do… Funny thing was, a job working for Wes while investigating the gator's gut feeling had an uplifting effect. *I'm employed.* Which was good for his new family. And he had a mystery to solve, which made him want to hum the theme from *Scooby Doo*—and eat a giant sandwich.

Damn that stupid pill he took to calm his nerves and halt any panic attacks. It totally fucked with his thought processes—and made him hungry, just like a certain weed he smoked in high school.

"When do I start?"

"Tonight. But not as a company man. I want us to do a sweep of the bayou by town."

"What's the swamp got to do with the stuff happening at the lab?" His eyes widened. "Are we looking for bodies?" *I hope not.* Nothing worse than coming across a corpse and having his croc go yum. Shudder.

"Looking for some of the missing folks is part of the reason. The other is that whatever screwed with Melanie is still out there. After dusk, I'll start from my place on the west side and move toward you."

"You want us to see if we can pinch that thing hiding out there."

"Or find a trace. I've done some patrols on my own, but I could use a second set of eyes."

"I can't believe we're going dinosaur hunting. Want me to keep an eye open for the wolfman, too?"

Wes didn't even crack a smile when he said, "I see you've gotten a bit of a recap of what's been sighted."

"A story about a wolfman kidnapping folks? Yeah. I heard it from my brother. But I'm less worried about the guy with a hair problem than I am of this dino thing people keep talking about. It went after my son last night." It still made Caleb's blood boil and run cold at the same time, given how close Luke had come to being snatched.

"That fucking lizard bastard gets around."

"You make it sound like you've encountered it before."

"In a sense." Swiveling in his seat, Wes turned to face a bank of monitors. "About a week ago, some of the institute's smokers said they saw something in the bayou. I'll be honest, since they were human"— because most shifters tended to shy from anything with flame and smoke—"I thought maybe they'd sniffed some swamp gasses. I mean, a walking lizard man? Sounds fucking crazy, except turns out it's true. Check out what I spotted on one of the surveillance cameras."

With a few rapid taps on a keyboard, a screen, showing a very boring white hallway, changed to another view. Given the greenish cast to the surroundings, it was easy to surmise the video was filmed at night. As to the setting, the empty concrete bay of a loading dock.

"This is so fascinating," Caleb couldn't resist saying.

"Fuck off and watch." The time stamp zoomed ahead, and suddenly something lurched into view. Human eyes in an alien face stared into the camera a quick moment only before it loped away.

Dropped jaw, meet floor. Caleb couldn't say a thing as Wes mumbled.

"Shit, I went too far. Hold on a second." Wes rewound, and Caleb leaned forward, intent on confirming what he thought he'd seen.

Bare pavement, illuminated by a light above the bay door. A barren spot circled by darkness, a darkness that birthed motion.

At the edge of the circle of light, a body lumbered into view. Two legs, one thicker than the other, the skinny one pale and shod in a shoe, while the other was bare and definitely not sporting piggly little toes. The creature had a long torso, dark in color with two arms. A misshapen figure that loped close to the loading dock and paused for a moment to peek up, big eyes, human eyes, staring at the lens taping it.

Human eyes in a monstrous face.

"Holy fucking hell, it is a lizard man."

Or to a child, a dinosaur since it walked upright and kept its arms tight to its sides.

Slowing the video, Wes took it frame by frame to the moment the ghastly visage stared at the camera. No mistaking the baleful glare in the eyes.

The frame froze.

"What the hell is that?" Caleb asked.

"A hybrid of some sort."

"Well, duh. I get that, but how?" While the species could interbreed, with the exception of some big cat species, hybrid crosses just didn't happen.

A bear and a wolf mated, the child was one or the other. A gator took up with a feline, the child, again, was one or the other. But this thing on the screen...

"It's got a beak. And I think that this here"— Wes leaned forward and traced the outline of a shape over its shoulder—"is a wing."

"Are you implying it's a bloody dragon?" Caleb couldn't help it, he laughed.

Wes scowled. "I don't know what the fuck it is. Just like I don't know where the fuck it lives. But I do know it's screwing with the people in town."

That was a sobering reminder. "Haven't you been able to track it? It's got a pretty distinctive scent."

"A scent that disappears into thin air in the middle of the swamp. Not a tree in sight. Nothing. Not even a footprint in the mud."

Caleb's turn to frown. From a young age, everyone recognized the Mercers as some of the best trackers around. People whispered they had to know how to hunt in order to feed all those bastard mouths.

But even if they didn't do it by necessity, the skill was inherent, and one that Caleb respected. Unlike the canine or feline breeds, reptiles like Wes and himself were at a disadvantage on land. While their eyesight and hearing were quite excellent, their sense of smell wasn't as developed as, say, a wolf's.

However, what the nose couldn't smell, the eyes could see, and if Wes said the tracks stopped dead, Caleb had no reason to disbelieve him, even if it seemed farfetched.

"That's why you want me to help you tonight. But surely you could have asked someone else."

"I did."

"And?" Caleb prodded.

"It didn't end up well." No mistaking the flash of pain in Wes's eyes, a quick glimpse that transformed into anger.

This was personal for Wes. "Who else has gone looking for it?"

"A few of us. We've been keeping the news on the down low so we don't scare people."

"Who's us?"

"Me, my brother. Daryl. There are a few others, but like I said, we've been keeping it on the down low."

"Which seems like a stupid idea. I mean, if there's something out there targeting shifters, shouldn't we be letting the whole town know and forming a posse to go after it?"

"You'd think that would be a good plan." A wry smile twisted Wes's lips. "Except the fellow who tried to organize a town meeting went missing."

"And you let that stop you?"

"No. I stopped when the second guy, my brother, went missing, too."

"Your brother? Which one?"

"Gary."

"He was two grades behind us, right?"

"Yeah. He disappeared on his way into town on his motorcycle. Hasn't been seen since."

"I'm sorry, dude." Caleb truly was. No matter his issues with Wes, he wouldn't wish that kind of loss on anyone.

"Yeah, well, Ma and my sisters took it hardest. I think the worst part is not knowing if he fucked off and said screw the town and its problems. Or if something happened to him."

"What's your gut say?"

"That he's alive and in trouble."

"If you think his disappearance is related to the shit happening, why not scream it from the rooftops? Why stay quiet?"

"Because I won't risk my sisters or mother. If the town council is in on the disappearances, then I don't want to tip my hand. As far as they know, I dropped the whole thing. Only me, your brother, and Daryl really know shit. And a few cousins, but they won't say shit and report only to me."

"And lucky me, I got invited to the party." Caleb couldn't help but chuckle. "Well, don't I feel warm and fuzzy. Hoping the town's dino monster will get me, too?"

"I was hoping you'd get taken by crotch rot, but no such luck. But more seriously, I need your help. Anything that can take out my brother is dangerous to us all. More disturbing is the fact that, whatever is going on, someone is willing to go to extremes to keep it secret."

Which meant it was up to them to figure it out.

And stop it.

Chapter Fourteen

It was ridiculous to be so excited about seeing Caleb pull into the front yard with her battered car. Chiding herself, though, didn't stop the giddy thrill that made her pulse speed up as she focused her gaze on him.

Unlike Renny, Luke didn't worry about appearing too eager to see Caleb. With his little legs pumping, he ran at Caleb, who swept him into his arms and flung him in the air.

Renny squeaked. Luke squealed. Caleb laughed.

"Got ya!" Caleb exclaimed, catching their son with ease. Never mind that Renny might have lost a few years off her life.

Get used to it. Daddies don't do things the same as mommies.

With Luke secured on his hip, instead of at the mercy of gravity, Caleb approached.

Her pulse fluttered. Excited. Scared.

She couldn't make up her mind.

Uncertainty still prevailed when it came to how she felt about the ease and speed Luke had taken to his father. The resentment she'd long harbored at Caleb's apparent abandonment seemed to be having a hard time taking root. Anger, much like fine sand, slipped through her grasp. Its departure left a hole quickly filled by anticipation.

And let's not forget heat.

Each time Renny ran into Caleb, the more difficult it became to remember the loneliness of life before he returned. He brought color into her world. Other than Luke, what did she have that made her want to smile for the simple joy of it?

He makes me happy.

Enjoying his presence, though, didn't mean she took to orders very well, and she could see by the frown knitting his brow they were about to have words about it. Good. Because it was time he learned the ground rules. Her rules.

Rule number one, she wasn't going to bow meekly.

Stopping a few feet from her, Caleb took in her appearance. Slightly grubby, given she'd spent the afternoon weeding the gardens while Luke played.

"Hi." She went for cheerful. Maybe it would temper his glower.

"Don't you hi me. What are you doing outside?" he demanded.

"Getting fresh air and exercise." She bent a knee and did a lunge. She might be a few pounds heavy, but she remained limber.

He didn't seem impressed. "I told you to stay in the house with Luke."

Nothing could have stopped her snort. "I'd like to see you entertain an active four-year-old penned in a house with no toys or kids' movies on a sunny day."

"You're his mother. You should have ordered it."

Caleb had a lot to learn when it came to parenthood. She laughed. "I'd like to see you try, and then enforce it. It is rather funny, too, coming from you, given you're the guy who barely spent time indoors. Weren't you like a master at escape?" She'd once overheard Caleb's mother at school lamenting to another parent that, short of duct taping them to a wall or gluing their feet to the floor, the boys just wouldn't stay still.

Apparently a reminder that Luke took after Caleb wasn't a good enough excuse. He clamped his lips tight. "This isn't funny. I told you to stay inside in order to keep you guys safe. Do you realize what could have happened if that thing came back and I wasn't here to protect you?"

"No, I don't know what might have happened because we have no idea what we came across yesterday. It could have been a monkey, fresh from a swamp mud bath, on the loose from the zoo. Maybe he wanted to come inside for a bath." The silly example saw a little chuckle slip from Luke.

"Or it could have been some sick predator that wouldn't be scared off by conventional means. You could have been hurt!" His body shook, and not with anger, she noted, but…fear?

Caleb truly was scared for them.

She might have given him some slack, except he did the unforgivable. He scared Luke.

A tremble went through their son. Her turn to glare. "You stop that naysaying right now, Caleb. You're scaring Luke. And I won't have it. What happened last night was a fluke. Probably some bayou animal looking for food scraps."

"Because you know a lot of animals who can open windows," he drawled with the utmost sarcasm.

No, but she wouldn't back down now. "Raccoons are pretty wily." And hey, the monkey idea wasn't that farfetched. It could happen. Right?

"Except that wasn't a coon trying to get in his room last night."

Luke popped his head from Caleb's shoulder to utter, "The dinosaur was coming for me. But he didn't come here. Grandma said he wouldn't, and if he did, she'd—"

"Fill its snout with salt rock," Claire announced with a thump of her shotgun on the front porch. "So stop harassing the girl, Caleb. The boy needed air. He was never in any danger. I was watching along with Princess."

The dog, upon hearing its name, sprang from the clump of marigolds in the flowerbed with a bark that startled Caleb into taking a step back, and that made Luke laugh.

The struggle on Caleb's face was funny. Hard to frown in annoyance at getting surprised by a teeny tiny dog when it so evidently pleased their son.

With the tension broken, time to change the subject.

"How did the interview go?" Renny asked.

"I was hired. I start tomorrow as a security guard." He made a face.

"That's great. I hear the dental benefits are wicked."

"Nothing wrong with my bite, baby." A quick wink and a sexy smile brought heat to her cheeks.

"I've got a ten o'clock shift at the grocery store tomorrow. Do you need a ride into work? I can probably drop you off on the way to Luke's school. But we'll have to leave early."

The crossed arms over his chest didn't bode well. Welcome to fight number two. "You are not going to work."

"Oh, yes I am."

It didn't take the tension in his jaw for her to know things were going to get ugly. Apparently, Claire noted it, too.

"Luke, sweetie, why don't you come inside with me and test drive the cookies that just came out of the oven. I've got a cold glass of milk made for dipping."

With a wiggle that saw Caleb setting Luke down, her son went scampering off, leaving Renny alone with a seriously bristling male.

So very hot. But sexy or not, she was not about to back down. "I am going to work tomorrow, Caleb, whether you like it or not. The bills won't pay themselves."

"I know, which is why I got a job."

"Well la-de-da for you. But just so you know, I am not a charity case, and I'm not about to beg you for money."

"No one said you had to beg. I'm just doing what's right. A man is supposed to support his family."

"I'm sure your mother will appreciate that."

"Renny!" He barked her name as his agitation increased, but that was fine because she was getting agitated, too. "Why must you be so difficult?"

"Because I'd like to know who gave you permission to start making decisions for me."

"I'm just trying to do what's right."

"Awesome. Do it, but while you're at it, keep in mind I make my own decisions. You're not the boss of me." Which sounded kind of juvenile when spoken aloud.

"You're being stubborn."

"I'm being a woman."

He glared.

Planting a hand on her hip, Renny glared right back. "Go ahead. Have your hissy fit. Get it out of your system."

"Hissy fit? Is that what you call my effort to try and protect you and Luke?"

"You're right. It's more like a dictatorship. And I'm rebelling. Letting you back into my life doesn't mean you're suddenly in charge. I am."

"What about Luke? Don't I get a say?"

"Yes. But for the moment, the final choices are mine. I might eventually be able to forgive, but it might take longer to forget." Because some things, like betrayal, haunted a girl forever—and the remembrance of a kiss never went away.

She would have expected maybe an explosion about now. Frustration that she wouldn't just fall into his arms and obey without question.

Instead, Caleb chuckled, a low, rumbling sound that tickled her senses.

"What's so funny?" she asked.

"You. Us fighting. The girl I remembered would have never yelled at me."

"The girl you remembered learned to toughen up." Best he knew that now before things went further.

"I like it."

Well, that wasn't the answer she'd expected, and her surprise might have been what led to her being pulled without a protest into his arms.

161

Oh, just admit it. She wanted to be in his arms. Wanted his lips on hers caressing with that sensual languor only he provided.

His hands spanned her waist, and he lifted her with ease, giving her better and deeper access to his mouth.

Delicious.

The sensual slide of his tongue over hers sent shivers up and down her body.

She slid her arms around his shoulders, digging her fingers into his short hair, keeping him close.

One of his hands slid from her waist to cup a buttock. He might have made small growling sound against her lips. She nipped him in the hopes he'd do it again.

A small voice asked, "Why is Daddy grabbing Mommy's bum?"

Why indeed?

How about because she liked it?

Problem was, there wasn't any privacy to pursue it.

Ugh.

Chapter Fifteen

We really need a place of our own.

The thought started when Luke caught them making out in the front yard that resulted in Renny pulling away—with reluctance.

Noooo. I don't want to stop.

But he had to. Now wasn't the time to drag her off to bed or to grope her in the front yard. He was a father now, and while he might not have had one for long, he did know proper parents didn't make out in front of their kid—unless he wanted to scar them for life. Caleb still remembered his horror when his mom got pregnant with Constantine and he realized it meant his mother had—ugh—sex.

But Luke wasn't the only reason he couldn't just toss his woman over his shoulder and indulge in an afternoon of fun between the sheets. His mother and brother were also in the house, and while sneaking around as teenagers to have nookie was fun—and almost a sport—he was a man now. And this man wanted a bed and some privacy.

We need to get a place of our own. This mantra persistently repeated itself throughout the afternoon, hours spent learning how to properly play cars in the dirt—while making *vroom* noises. An educational day for someone who'd never been around children much.

The first thing he learned was they were bloody

inexhaustible. When Luke began to ask questions, they never ended, and after the seventh "Why?" in a row, he shot Renny a rescue-me look, only to have her giggle and walk away.

"I'll get you for that," he mock-threatened.

"I can't wait," was her saucy reply.

When his son ran off at one point to find some juice—Caleb having sent Luke to his mom—Caleb stalked Renny down. He found her lounging in a chair at the back of the house, protected from insects by the screened porch, reading a paperback.

"You'd make an awful soldier," he said as he cast a shadow over her.

She grinned up at him. "Why?"

"You left me behind under fire," he growled. "I barely made it through the barrage of questions."

"Just teaching you how to swim the same way my daddy did. Lucky for you, you didn't sink."

"So you think I did okay?" *Shoot me now.* He sounded like such a wuss for even asking. Given he needed to reassert his manliness, he sat on the end of her lounge chair, resulting in the other end flipping up and sending her tumbling into him.

"Caleb!" she squealed.

"That's what I like to hear," he said, shifting his weight so that the chair balanced out. He also kept her on his lap, where she belonged. "Although, if you're going to scream my name like that, the least you could do is get naked first."

"We can't get naked. Someone—"

"Might see," he finished with a sigh. "Being an adult blows."

"And so do I," she said with a wink. "What a

shame you'll have to wait for a sample."

Mind blown. The increased heart rate and heat flushing his skin? Pure fucking arousal. "You are being intentionally cruel. You do realize that, right?"

The smile on her lips turned, if possible, even naughtier. "Who, me? Would I punish you?"

"I hope so." He cupped the back of her head, his fingers digging into the soft mass of her hair. "Because I need to be punished. So I can kiss you for forgiveness."

She inhaled sharply a moment before his lips covered hers, sliding slow and sensually over them, hushing any retort she might have had.

But Renny didn't seem interested in denying him. She kissed him right back, more cruel punishment because he couldn't help but imagine those plush, pliant lips wrapped around a certain part of him. A hard part...

His erection pressed against his jeans, and he felt the seam of her shorts rubbing as she wiggled atop him.

A softly sighed sound was his ticket to deepen the kiss, the slick slide of his tongue along hers sending a shiver through her frame.

Her sensual responsive nature to his touch was another form of torturous tease. Her fingers dug into his back and her arms wound around him, folding him in her embrace. His own hands slid down and cupped her rounded buttocks. A perfect handful that he massaged.

The snap of her head breaking their kiss made him growl. "Get back here."

"We should stop," she panted.

"That's just being cruel." Since she wouldn't give him her lips, he dove in for a nibble at her throat.

Her fingers threaded his hair, tight, almost painful. He couldn't tell if she wanted him to stop his sensual nips or needed more…

More, of course.

He sucked at her skin, and she moaned, "You're playing dirty."

"And loving it. So are you." He could tell. She couldn't hide her arousal from him.

"But someone might see."

And those who might spy were family, and that meant he couldn't kill them.

Yet stopping…*I don't want to stop touching her.*

He rumbled against her skin.

"Caleb!" Said in a way that let him know he had to rein back his passion.

Pulling back from her, he let out a breath, a long, heavy sound. "When did I get old and worried about doing the right fucking thing?"

She smiled. "You matured. And just so you know"—she leaned close to whisper—"it's really, really sexy." She gave him one last lingering and sweet kiss that left him sitting there with eyes closed long after she fled. How emasculating was it to want to relive that moment in perpetuity?

For the first time in what seemed like forever, he felt complete. He'd found what was missing in his life, the last piece—no, not a piece, a person who could make him whole.

Make me happy.

Sappy shit. *I'd be happier if I had a bedroom with a lock.*

But that would come. He couldn't let his impatience rush things. He'd waited years to see Renny again. He could wait a few days longer. Besides, he knew one important thing now.

She still wants me.

Hesitation arising from the past might still come between them, but she was thawing, perhaps even forgiving him. Hope was a hot furnace to a body he thought ran cold-blooded.

"Why is Daddy sleeping while sitting up?"

Not sleeping but dreaming. With his eyes wide open about a future.

The rest of that day, the best Caleb could manage was a stolen kiss here and there that left Renny's cheeks flushed and her eyes bright.

The occasional touch kept his blood boiling while, at the same time, the inability to take things further frustrated him.

He couldn't even take them back to her place, not given he'd promised to meet Wes tonight. He didn't want her being alone, not until they knew this strange monster business was taken care of.

Keep them safe.

The mantra repeated itself over and over. He blamed it for the tremors that hit when he was away from Renny.

Separation? Bad.

He couldn't explain why, but he felt whole when with Renny. In control. Being with her gave him a purpose that had no room for panic.

He did what had to be done. He protected. He provided. He kissed…

Okay, that was less for her than it was for him.

The feel of her lips against his, her hands grasping at his nape, her skin feverish for his touch, the signs she wanted him were there. They bolstered him. Made him strong again.

Strong enough to tolerate the hunter in him wanting to rise for a peek.

I don't know if I want to let you out.

He spoke to his other side, knowing the croc already was aware of his trepidation. Whenever his reptile came out to play, blood ran.

Because that is the nature of the beast.

Something he heard over and over, but it didn't change how he felt. He could handle violence, but his croc self took it to a scary level, dragging him along for the ride, willing or not.

Practice makes perfect.

Did that really apply when dealing with another personality? Every time he let the croc out, he feared losing another part of himself. Of returning less human than before.

Yet, containing the beast didn't work. It still lurked in his head, tossing its own thoughts and emotions into everything Caleb did.

Remember what happened the last few times you tried to cage the beast?

Practice makes perfect. The expression repeated itself.

Stop whining about your split personality problem and get shifting. Full dusk had fallen, and Wes was expecting him, not as a man, but as a crocodile.

Fuck fear. Fear never helped a situation. *I will make fear my bitch.* Time to throw on the scales and do something that would make people, like his family, safe.

But before he did so, Caleb made sure his brother would stand guard in his stead. It involved a conversation that might have made more than a few humans blanch.

"I gotta go on the prowl and see what I can find out about that lizard thing lurking around," Caleb told Constantine after having tucked Luke in and saying goodnight to Renny—which involved more kissing and even bluer balls.

"You want me to curtail my evening of alcoholic debauchery to babysit?"

"Yeah."

Constantine shrugged. "Okay. But I'm telling you right now, if something pays us a visit, I'm not holding Princess back."

Casting a glance at the rat, who wore a pink bow today in her fine hair, Caleb smirked. "Sure, let the hound of hell loose. I'm sure your hairball will do a fine job hobbling any attackers with a rabid gnaw of their Achilles tendon."

"Laugh all you want, but she actually goes for the ankles so she can get her prey to bend over and present their jugular. Princess believes in going for the killing shot." Said with such pride.

Grrr. A tiny lip pulled back, a murderous glare entered those giant eyes, and her ears pointed in aggressive fury.

"There is something seriously deviant about that dog," Caleb said as he glanced again at Princess.

"I know." Constantine beamed. "Pure perfection."

At the words, Princess yipped, but Con missed the canine smirk on her tiny muzzle.

Much as I hate to admit it, that's one fucking smart appetizer.

With that kind of protection left behind for his family, Caleb stripped and walked naked to the edge of the bayou. He dipped a toe in the brackish water, delaying the inevitable. The water was fine. The humming mosquitoes didn't bother him. Not even the mud.

It was the *other* he dreaded.

So long since he'd allowed his feral side to rise. Months since he'd felt the gnawing ache of the hunger, the thrill of the beast as it pursued its prey. The chomp of—

He clamped his eyes shut. But for once, he couldn't stop the feelings. The alien thought process of his beast merged with his consciousness.

Remember what the shrink said.

Don't fight your animal side.

Don't equate what you do while shifted with who you are.

We are hunters. And hunters don't just chase their prey. Sometimes they eat them, too. It's the nature of life.

A life Caleb had tried to deny, worried that there was something wrong with him, that his monster took too much pleasure in the death of others.

But other than that first mistake, had he truly ever lost absolute control? The rest had all deserved what he dished.

Still, it only took one major mistake to fuck me over.

How much worse if the next fuckup happened to Renny or Luke?

But he couldn't think that way. Not now when he needed his senses sharp.

Tonight we hunt.

The lukewarm water bathed his scaled skin, and if a croc could sigh, his did. How he'd missed the smooth glide of his powerful body through the silky swamp. Vegetation tickled his underbelly, the waving fronds not impeding his progress. His sensory spots along his jaw fed him further information—temperature, current, the fact that this water lacked salt.

Maybe once this was over, he'd take his family to the beach. A day spent soaking in the sun and briny water, with Renny in a bikini.

His pleasant fantasy didn't stop him from doing his task.

Tail swishing, Caleb zigzagged across the submerged parts of the wetland. When he had to, he did a belly run across the ground, startling the smaller rodents into hiding.

Thankfully, his reptile did not feel a need to stop for a snack. He'd made sure to have a large dinner so his snaggletoothed side wouldn't be tempted.

With that fear quelled, he found a lot more enjoyment in the bayou search. He spent hours crisscrossing the marshy acres between his house and the Bittech Institute. Nothing. Nothing. *Ooh, fresh turtle eggs.* Nothing.

He was just about to call it quits when he detected it. Another large predator.

Inching up onto the muddy shore, Caleb stayed low, his belly brushing the ground as he took in the situation. He crept forward, frame held high enough to not drag and alert his target. He slitted his eyes, filtering the ambient starlight to guide his steps.

Silently, he moved, the predator facing away

from him, upwind, providing a tempting target. Caleb opened his mouth wide, his long, extended snout ridged with sharp teeth. He snapped it shut with a *clack*.

Wes didn't even jump. "Dude, you are seriously loud. Like my brother"—a bull gator—"in a china shop. Did you really think I wouldn't hear you coming?"

It took but a moment to shift shapes, a gasping process that he didn't really enjoy. The youngsters always asked as they approached those puberty years, "Does it hurt?"

Hell yeah, but you got used to it. And if you didn't, you lied so you wouldn't look like a pussy.

Straightening from his crouch, Caleb replied. "I take it you didn't find anything." A few strides brought Caleb to a different fallen trunk to sit on because while nudity might be acceptable among shifters, getting into someone's naked space, unless you were banging them, was considered rude.

"A faint scent trace. But it was old and didn't lead anywhere."

"Are we sure that thing is hiding in the swamp?"

"Where else would it be?" Wes asked. "It's not as if it can rent a room in town."

"So I guess we keep looking."

"Not tonight we aren't. You have a job to get to tomorrow morning."

Caleb rolled his eyes. "I guess I wouldn't want to piss off the boss the first day."

"You got that straight."

For a moment, they sat in silence and let the sounds of the bayou roll over them. The soft plop of water as something surfaced for a bite. The hum of insects out for a night of drinking blood and procreating before the dawn saw them dying. The chorus of frogs, their symphony interrupted every now and then as one of their number went from entertainment to dinner.

"Fucking hell, I gotta ask. Why did you leave?"

Wes's question startled Caleb, and he shot the other man a look. "Why do you care?"

"I don't. I was just surprised is all. Especially given how hot and heavy you were with Renny."

"Something happened, and I kind of had no choice."

"I know what you did that summer." Wes smirked.

Caleb froze. "What are you talking about?" The words emerged from a dry mouth. Caleb had been alone when it happened. And he still wasn't sure what had happened. A blank spot resided in his mind. One minute he was walking home from Renny's, and then, in what felt like a blink, he regained awareness as his jaws were ripping apart a man.

"Considering you left not even twelve hours after you were dumped in the marsh with that dead guy—"

"Stop. What do you mean dumped with a dead guy? What the hell did you see?"

The hard look Wes shot him held a glint of red, the beast he held within but seemed to share his life with in harmony.

"I mean that a couple of guys dragged your scaly sleeping ass out of a big truck and dropped you in the water and then dumped a body in front of you. Some guy wearing army scrubs with a syringe stuck you and ran away. He and the others took off in the truck before you woke up."

Woke up hungry, dazed, and angry. He'd smelled something in front of him and snapped. Chewed. *I killed and ate a human.*

He'd later retched most of it up on shore when he staggered from the marsh, naked and dirty. But the military truck, with its blazing lights and barking soldiers, seemed to know what he was, and what he was guilty of.

Of course they did because… "I was framed." Caleb couldn't help a note of incredulity. "Those fucking assholes framed me. They made me think I'd lost control. They told me I killed a man." The cry he let loose held frustrated fury. All those years he'd blamed himself. Feared himself. Done despicable things because they said he had to. "It was all a fucking lie. And I believed it." Instead of trusting himself.

"I would have told you what I saw back then, but before I could get to you, you were gone. You and a few other boys. You're the only one that came back."

Because shifters were the expendable soldiers, the ones sent into the most dangerous of situations because they were the most likely to survive. "Lucky me."

"Oh, stop it with the pity-me, I'm-so-screwed routine. At least you came back. Can those other guys say the same?"

"No." He'd lost too many friends to count. "But it's hard to forget."

"You don't have to forget. But you can choose to live in the now and create new memories, good ones to remember."

"This is getting way too Kumbaya for me," Caleb growled.

"Don't worry, I was going to mock your dick size in a second."

"And there is so much to mock. I tell you, it's hard carrying that kind of weight around, but the ladies love it."

Wes burst out laughing. "Asshole."

"And I'm a fucking brain-addled tool obviously because, crazily enough, I missed this."

"Missed hunting possibly murderous dinos in the swamp?"

A snicker left Caleb. "Actually, I'm liking this new game." So long as he won in the end. "But more, I missed home. The swamp. A place I can let my croc out that has nothing to do with the war or taking out the enemy."

"They really did a number on you."

"And then some."

But he was healing and, even better, falling in love all over again, which came with a new set of anxieties.

Was his family safe while he was gone?

His chat with Wes over, Caleb took a direct route back to his house, anxious to check on them. What if the creature they hunted had circled back and gone after Luke again?

What if…

Curse it, now he was the one who couldn't stop questioning.

Body undulating, he moved and grooved his way home only to pause at the muddy edge.

Someone is watching.

He almost stayed hidden in the weeds, willing them to go, but that smacked of cowardice.

Striding from the brackish water, he immediately scented the air, but it remained clear of alien odors.

In other good news, the house remained secure. The traps he'd strung along the window intact, the doors closed, and he assumed locked. Nothing seemed out of place.

Everything looked and smelled right except for him. The swamp's perfume clung to his skin, a miasma he would never dare bring into the house. A wooden spoon named Spanky had taught him that lesson young.

Besides, he didn't need to go inside to get clean, not when they had an outdoor shower that drew from their well. It wasn't hot water, but it was fresh, and the bar of soap kept in a dish, lemon scented.

It didn't take long to rinse the bayou from his skin, but even once clean, he didn't move. He remained standing under the spray, face lifted to it, and tried not to react as she drew near.

Renny.

From the moment he'd risen from the waters, he'd sensed her presence and tried not to let on. It wasn't easy, not when he knew she watched.

She sees my beast.

A part of him had wanted to submerge under the murky surface of the swamp. To hide who he was. What he was.

More secrets.

He couldn't do it. If he wanted a life with Renny, they needed to start with honesty, starting with his croc.

This is who I am. Whom he'd never dared reveal back when they were dating. Would she run away?

He might have held his breath when he rose from the weeds and mud, scaled skin rippling and sliding as the magic of the change drew his reptilian features back to the spot hidden within. Smooth flesh, strands of hair, and a face that could pass for human took their place. He walked as a man, straight, proud, and naked.

Did he forget to mention aroused? Knowing she watched, and didn't flee, brought a boil to his blood. He could suntan himself under the heat of her gaze.

But he pretended to not know. *Don't push her.* Let her come to him.

Please let her come to me.

Feeling her stare the entire time he showered did nothing to help his erection. How hard it was—so very, very hard—to not stroke himself to completion. But he didn't dare.

She watched. What would she think if he came without her?

Would she know that he thought of her? Would it disgust her? What if it didn't? What if he spent himself and she needed him?

Pretending nonchalance was so difficult and remembering to breathe as she approached with soft footsteps even harder.

"You can stop faking it. I know that you know I'm here."

He turned to face her, unable to stop a smile. "Say that fast five times."

"I've better ideas if you're in the mood for

tongue twisting." Despite the droplets of water hitting her from the spray, she remained close to him. Very close.

The tank top she wore molded the curves of her breasts, outlining their weighted roundness and delineating nipples that shriveled into points as he stared at them.

Tiny shorts hugged her shapely hips, and a hint of rounded belly peeked at him between those skimpy bottoms and top.

"What are you doing outside?"

"Waiting for you."

At his growled "baby," she stepped closer and put a finger on his lips. "Don't get mad. I didn't do anything stupid. I watched from the window until I was sure it was you."

"Just because you see a croc doesn't mean it's me."

"Princess didn't bark."

"But I might."

She slid closer, getting wet in the lukewarm water jetting from the wide rain showerhead. "While I appreciate the intent behind the bark, I think I prefer"—she leaned up on tiptoe to rub her lips against his—"the bite."

He met her partway and was rewarded with the edge of her teeth grasping his lower lip and tugging.

Because he was apparently an idiot, he had to ask, "What are you doing?"

"What does it look like I'm doing?" she whispered with a soft laugh against his lips.

"It looks like you're seducing me."

"Only looks like?" she teased with another

nibble of his mouth.

"Feels like, too." He slid his arms around her, drawing her tight to him and deepening the kiss.

For a moment, their hot breaths mingled, their bodies pressed.

Then he groaned and pulled away. He grasped her hands and held them away from him, ignoring her sounds of protest.

"Stop, baby."

"Stop? Why? I want this. Heck, you want this." She punctuated her words with a grind of her hips against him.

His resolved wavered, and he forced himself to breathe as he looked her in the face.

Her perfect face.

How did I get so lucky to have a chance to start over? A chance to have a new life, a true life, with the woman he loved. But, if he ever had any hope of making it work, he needed to start it with honesty.

"You need to know the truth. About why I left."

And that quickly, the soft smile on her lips faded and her body tensed. "What happened to you can't tell?"

"I can't. At least I'm not supposed to. But…" Caleb sighed as he leaned back against the post that held the plumbing for the shower. He shrugged and smiled. "I never claimed I was a good boy. Sometimes, rules need to be broken."

"Will you get in trouble?" She touched his cheek. "You don't have to tell me if it might harm you."

"The people I swore to, they're not around

anymore. And even if they were, they already did their worst when they took me from you. Fucking bastards, using me and lying to me, they never gave a damn about me, only what I could do for them." He caught her gaze. "But you gave a damn. You loved me, and instead of respecting that, I chose to keep a promise to some asshats who probably wouldn't piss on me if I was on fire." On the contrary, after the embarrassment of their mission overseas, most would have preferred he died, keeping their secrets intact.

She traced a finger down the scar until the tip of her digit ran across his lower lip. He nipped it. As if he could resist. "You don't have to tell anymore. I know you, Caleb. I might have been angry, but deep down, a part of me knew you wouldn't have left unless you had a damned good reason."

"I did. I murdered someone. Or thought I had."

He waited for it. The recoil, the horror, the quizzical...

"And?"

And? He blinked at her. "And I said I killed someone. Or at least I thought my croc had."

"Thought? Is there doubt about what happened?"

"More like a revelation." He explained quickly what he thought had happened and then Wes's version. All the while he got them out of the shower. He procured two towels from the weather-proof chest beside it.

Wrapping Renny first, he carried her to the picnic table and seated her on its top. He didn't move far away, but rather paced in short strides in front of her.

He couldn't explain the relief that she was listening instead of running. He'd expected several reactions from her, hell, he'd experienced many himself as he lived the past few years, but Renny took his tale without flinching.

When he finished, she tilted her head to look at him. "Sounds like it was a rough time."

"Very."

"But I have a question for you. How could you have thought you killed a man for no cause? I know you, Caleb. You would have never done something like that."

"Wouldn't I? Every time I let the croc out, it feeds. On live things. From the moment I met you, I was afraid I'd scare you off, that the beast would repulse you."

"It's part of who you are."

"A part I always struggled with."

"Why didn't you tell anyone?"

He shrugged. "Tell who? My mom? She already had enough stress without me whining about being weirded out by my croc's antics."

"What about your friends? Their fathers?"

"In case you've forgotten, I'm a guy. Asking for help is like asking for directions. We just don't do it. Especially back then. I was an arrogant little fucker. I didn't want to ask anyone because I didn't want to look weak."

"Nobody would have thought that. Actually, I take that back. Wes would have mocked you, probably Daryl, too, but they were your peers. They would have teased, but they would have helped."

"Wes was never my peer." Rival, yes, and one

181

Caleb never admired, even if he bought the same studded leather coat within a day of hearing about the gator's.

"Whatever you want to call those guys, they would have had your back."

"I know that now." Hindsight was more than twenty-twenty. It was a bitch that taunted.

Renny wasn't done. Her brow knitted into lines as she thought aloud. "According to Wes, it was a setup, and I'll be honest, a pretty obvious one, it seems. I mean, didn't you think it was weird that those guys who stopped you knew so much about you and what happened?"

"Well, yeah, it seemed strange, but things went so fast." He'd also still been reeling at the time, from the shock and, he now realized, lingering effects from drugs making his thought process murky. "They said they knew what I'd done. They threatened to arrest me. To expose me, as a matter of fact." *You're a monster that should pay for his crimes.* "Unless I would agree to a deal."

"A deal that involved you fighting for them."

"Obey. Fight. Kill. The choice was join the military and depart immediately for a mission or have not just myself exposed, but my family, too."

Caleb had stopped to stand in front of her. It was simple for her to lean forward so she might cup his face with both hands. "Oh, Caleb." Moisture brightened her gaze, and he could feel his throat tighten.

"I—" He swallowed. "I was a coward and agreed. Instead of being willing to face what I'd done, I agreed to their terms and left."

He dropped his eyes to stare down, but she

wouldn't let him escape. She ducked under and forced him to see her expression.

"You had no choice."

"I could have said no and taken what I deserved."

"You protected your family. This town."

"I deserted you."

"To do the right thing. The hard thing." She brushed her lips across his as she whispered, "I forgive you."

Had someone shot him? Had an axe severed his legs? What else could explain the slump of his knees? The rough seating at the picnic table pressed against his joints. Head bowed, he leaned forward and pressed his face against Renny's belly as he wrapped his arms around her legs.

His body shook. Not quite with tears, more like relief. His heart swelled with love. Hope blossomed in his soul. So many feelings assailed him. Emotions long pent up, thought dead, pressed him in all directions, and yet, in some respects, he felt lighter.

He'd told the truth, and the chains it bound him with no longer held him down.

"Caleb." Softly spoken. She lifted his chin and let him see the love in her gaze. "Kiss me."

He rose to his feet and, in a smooth motion, clasped her to him. Dipping his head, he claimed her lips, trying to show how he felt.

But the taste of her wasn't enough… He wanted all of her.

He pulled away and groaned.

"Where are you going?"

"I need a cold shower."

"Whatever for?"

He spun to face her. "Because if I don't, then I'm going to strip that towel from you and lick every goddamned inch of your luscious body."

"What's stopping you?"

"In case you haven't noticed, we still don't have a bloody room." Who would have ever thought he'd pray for privacy?

"It's almost one a.m. No one is awake but you and me." She leaned back on her elbows and let her knees fall open, the motion undoing the simple tuck of the towel. As its edges peeled away, it revealed the swell of her breasts, the sharp tips of her nipples, and the shadowy cleft between her thighs.

He might have been punched to the head one too many times, but that didn't make him stupid. Caleb didn't wait for another invitation.

He dove on the offering, his hands spanning her waist, an hourglass indent made for holding. His mouth claimed hers, but it didn't remain long, not with the luscious temptations waiting below.

The swirl of his tongue around a brazen peak drew forth a cry from her. And another when he let the flat edge of his teeth tug. He sucked her breasts into his mouth, enjoying the pull on her flesh, the scrabble of her nails on his shoulders and how her heels dug into the base of his spine as she tried to draw him nearer.

He held firm—and he meant *firm*—and kept his teasing play of her nipples, switching back and forth until she just moaned continuously.

Then he blazed a trail down her rib cage to the round softness of her belly. He rubbed his bristled jaw against her skin and felt the shiver that went through her.

He wasn't done with his journey.

Farther his lips stroked, their feathery path leading to one plump thigh. He couldn't help but nibble.

Yummy.

But something even tastier beckoned.

"Open for me," he whispered against her mound. Her legs were parted, but he wanted more. He wanted to see the source of her musky honey.

She lay right back against the picnic tabletop, golden hair spread around her, chest rising and falling as she panted her arousal. She drew her legs farther apart, bringing her heels to rest and grip the edge of the table. She offered herself to him, and he trembled.

She is so damned beautiful. How could I possibly think I deserve her?

He didn't. But he would do his damnedest to do right by her.

Caleb leaned forward and blew hotly on her cleft. The petals to her sex shivered. The heady scent of her arousal surrounded him. The taste of her burst upon his tongue with only one lap.

Sweet ambrosia. He licked her sex with a rumbling enjoyment, an enjoyment she shared and expressed with her moaned, "Caleb."

He parted her nether lips, stabbing his tongue into her heat, feeling the erotic tension permeating her body. He wanted her to come.

Fingers replaced his tongue, a pair to stretch her tight channel while his tongue flicked at her hooded clitoris, causing it to swell so that each stroke made her gasp.

Her pussy tightened around his fingers.

He grabbed her clit with his lips.

Her hips arched off the table.

Pumping fingers and teasing lips followed. She drew in a sharp breath. Her body bowed, she could only gasp, no real sound escaping her.

The final, hard clamp of her channel made him gasp and then exult as her pussy convulsed in climactic waves for him. Yet still, he pushed his fingers in her, drawing it out and then rebuilding it as he found her sweet spot. And stroked it.

Stroked her sensitive G-spot until she was panting and squirming again. But this time, he wasn't content with just fingers. His cock bobbed, hard and ready.

The tip of it butted against her plump lips, slid between them, and then he slammed into her as she wrapped her legs around his flanks and drew him in.

His turn to cry out. "Aah." The sensation of molten heat engulfing him was too much for him to resist.

When she would have grabbed at him, he manacled her wrists in his hands and drew them over her head, stretching her on the table. He held her pinned as he stroked into her.

Long.

Hard.

Deep.

She shuddered even as he retreated.

Then slammed back in, making her cry out.

Pull back. Then in.

Caleb thrust into Renny, his body rigid as he controlled his pleasure. But he wouldn't be able to hold it for long. She was just too exquisite.

Even though he held her hands prisoner, she still managed to drive him wild, arching her hips to take him deep, the walls of her sex squeezing so tight.

He kept moving firmly, trying to remain conscious of the fact that she lay on a table, not a bed. He had to be gentle with her.

But their passion wasn't cooperating.

Without conscious volition, Caleb quickened his pace. He wrapped an arm around her waist and pulled her to a seated position with her ass still on the towel. His strokes got shorter but harder. They banged deep within her sheath.

She clenched around him. Her body pulsed with heat and energy. She buried her face in the crook of his neck and shoulder. The moment before she climaxed, she said the most incredible thing, "You're mine," and then she did the most mind-blowing thing.

She bit him and, for all intents and purposes, made him hers.

Chapter Sixteen

The picnic table wasn't the most comfortable bed, but when they finished making love, neither was ready to separate. Problem was a light rain made it unpleasant to stay outside. So she'd entered the house and cuddled Caleb on the couch. Just for a little while.

Or so she'd thought until she heard the little voice saying, "Mommy, why are lying on top of Daddy?" On the list of awkward questions, that one ranked pretty high, along with "Why are you wearing Daddy's shirt?"

Somehow, explaining that she'd lost hers because she'd gone out to seduce Caleb didn't seem appropriate. She stammered out a white lie. "Mine got wet."

"Very wet," Caleb added, completely deadpan.

"Oh. Okay." And with that, her son wandered away and was soon making truck noises.

She, on the other hand, was making embarrassed groaning ones.

Caleb rubbed her back. "Now, now, baby, it's not that bad. At least we were wearing clothes."

He laughed harder when she elbowed him. Rolling off, she tugged down his shirt, which came to a respectable mid-thigh, and then marched off toward the bathroom.

It didn't take a peek over her shoulder to know

Caleb admired the view, and must have been pretty blatant about it because Luke asked, "Why are you so happy, Daddy?"

"Because I have you and your mom."

She might have stumbled. Stupid ledge between the bathroom floor and the hall.

That morning, Caleb was treated to the hustle and bustle of a family that needed to get ready to get out the door, on time. Luke had to be at school before nine, and then it was time to drop Caleb off with a kiss, then on to her own boring job at the grocery store.

Ho hum.

Until that night when she and Caleb snuck out for a tryst in his brother's truck. They steamed the windows that night.

Broke the picnic table the next.

Made use of the outdoor shower…

Each morning she woke to Luke's grin and Caleb's hug.

It was wonderful.

So the week went, and despite the lack of privacy, and the glower on Caleb's face each time she went to work, she was happy.

On Thursday about mid-afternoon, a familiar tingle let her know Caleb was there. She turned around to find him standing at the bottom end of her checkout aisle.

He wore the official Bittech uniform, and it suited him. She especially wanted to strip it from him.

I will…later.

"What are you doing here so early?" she asked. "I'm not due to finish for another hour."

"Wes let me off early so I could show you a

surprise."

"It will have to wait. My boss will never let me leave early." She made a face. "But in other news, I'm not working tonight."

"How come?"

"The club is shut down on account of a burst water pipe in the bathroom."

"I don't suppose it could stay shut forever," he grumbled.

But that was all he was doing. Grumbling. He might not like her job at the Itty Bitty Club, but they'd come to an understanding. While Claire and Constantine—with his sly Chihuahua—watched Luke at night, Caleb kept an eye on Renny at work. Just not in the club and it wasn't because Caleb had an inability to, as he stated it, "Watch guys hit on my girl." Nope, he stayed outside because she requested it.

In a funny twist, Renny found herself really uncomfortable with mostly naked women strutting around him. Not that they dared try anything.

The dancers learned, after the first time he popped in for a beer, to keep their hands off. Whoever thought human women were meek never saw Renny grab a girl by the hair and growl, "Keep your paws off my man, Tina, or I will make your furry ass into a rug."

Because where Caleb was concerned, now that he was back, he was hers. And nothing, *nothing* would keep her away from him.

Although some idiots seemed intent on trying, like her boss at the supermarket who barked, "Suarez, why aren't you working?"

Renny rolled her eyes before facing her manager, some guy sent down by head office to maximize the store's revenue. "Work doing what?" She swept a hand toward her empty aisle. "There's no one here, Benny." Indeed, the few shoppers in the store had yet to finish and need a check out.

"Maybe there's no one on account someone is too high and mighty to do her job because she's too busy yapping."

She clamped her lips tight. There wasn't much she could say to placate Benny.

But Caleb didn't know that. "It's my fault. I was the one who came in and talked to her."

If Caleb thought to diffuse the situation, he was wrong because the manager of the store didn't care. Benny also didn't realize when he took a step forward and aimed his florid face and vitriol at Caleb just who he was dealing with.

"Listen, you scarred freak. I don't need your type coming in here and scaring off my clients."

Renny might take a lot of flack at the hands of this miserable excuse for humanity, but like heck would she let him berate Caleb.

"Don't you dare talk to him like that." She came around the counter and stood before Caleb, who appeared surprised.

"It's okay, Renny. I'm gonna have to get used to hearing shit like that."

"No, it is not okay. You got those scars serving your country, and now this moron thinks he can insult you. Not happening."

"Watch your mouth or you'll be looking for another job." Benny tried to look intimidating, but a human had nothing on the real predators she'd grown up with.

"Are you threatening to fire me? No need." She fumbled at the buttons holding her red vest closed. Renny balled the fabric and tossed it at Benny. "I quit." Turning to Caleb, she smiled. "Looks like I'm finished early after all. Let's go see that surprise."

"You can't quit," Benny hollered after her.

Renny stuck up a certain finger over her shoulder.

"Did you just tell him to fuck off in sign language?" Caleb asked. "That is so freaking sexy."

"Weirdo."

"Your weirdo, baby. Now are you ready?"

"For what?"

"You'll see," was his enigmatic reply.

What she saw was an overgrown front lawn and a tiny house whose wooden shingles were grayed from the weather and, in places, green from humidity. But the windows were intact if bare of curtains.

Inside, the wide plank floor had lost its varnish, but it was swept clean. Renny peeked around the space. The open living room with its sliding glass door to the backyard of the house. The kitchen with its white tile countertops and painted cabinets.

"Why are we here?" she asked, already guessing.

"Say hello to our home."

"Our?" she asked as she spun with an arched brow. "Kind of presumptuous, don't you think?"

He looked crestfallen. "Yes, ours. I mean, after the week we've spent, and—"

She placed a finger on his lips and laughed. "I'm sorry. I shouldn't tease you like that. Of course I want to be here with you."

"Luke, too."

A snicker escaped her. "Well, duh. We're kind of a package deal."

He made a face. "I am so bad at this relationship stuff."

She draped her arms around his neck and smiled. "Oh, I don't know about that. So far you're doing pretty damned good. So good, I think we should test out this place before we grab our son and move in with our stuff."

They made love that afternoon on the countertop. In the shower. And were now curled together with naked limbs in a nest on the floor.

For once, there was no rush to be anywhere. Not even to pick up Luke because Caleb had already made arrangements with Melanie. Since her best friend had to go see Bittech for her fertility test results, she'd drop Luke off on her way home after grabbing a bite for dinner, giving Renny and Caleb some alone time.

From the direction of her purse, her phone jangled, a catchy ditty titled, "I'm Going Bananas," an old Madonna song she'd bought and used as a ringtone for Melanie

Rolling away from Caleb, Renny said over her shoulder on her way to grab it, "She's probably looking for details."

"I thought women weren't supposed to gossip about their sex lives," he said, rolling to his back and lacing his hands under his head. It pulled at his flesh and defined some of his muscles. The scar that twisted down his side did nothing to mar his perfection. Rather it drew her eye more to the beauty of his shape.

It also distracted. She fished the phone out of her purse just as it went to voicemail. Before she could redial, it was ringing again.

She answered with a laugh. "Holy having a cow, Melanie, are you that impatient to hear the details?"

"Renny, he's gone." Said in a voice tight with fear.

The world stopped spinning, and Renny's whole bearing froze as she made sense of the words.

As if from a distance, she heard herself say, "What do you mean he's gone?"

"Luke. He's missing. The twins say the dinosaur got him."

"No." Renny whispered the word through numb lips. All of her went limp, including her fingers, which released the phone. Her knees decided to no longer support her, dumping her to the floor, where she hit hard. But the pain of impact was nothing compared to that gripping her heart.

Chapter Seventeen

As soon as Renny said, "What do you mean he's gone?" Caleb was moving, yet his fastest speed wasn't fast enough to catch her before she collapsed. He dropped to the floor beside Renny, drawing her into his lap even as he dove for the phone.

He tucked it to his ear as he held a sobbing Renny close. "Tell me what's happened."

It didn't take long. Through hiccupping sobs, Melanie let him know what had happened. In a nutshell, Luke was gone.

Taken.

Because I wasn't there to protect him.

It didn't take any kind of medical degree in psychology to see Renny blamed herself for Luke's disappearance. There was plenty of blame to go around, starting with his own.

Damn me for not remaining more vigilant. He'd let his guard down after a week of no sightings. He, Wes, and even Daryl had done some more patrols, but found nothing. Not a single whiff of its unique aroma, not a peep from anyone in town. They'd wondered if the creature had moved on or was dead. Or perhaps it hadn't posed a threat at all.

In his cocoon of happiness, he'd allowed himself to relax, and now, because of his mistake, his son had paid the price.

Unfair!

Caleb slammed the steering wheel as he was forced to stop for a red light. He might have run it, but he somehow doubted the car would win in the battle for space against the rather large dump truck.

"This is all my fault." He growled. "I should have waited until later to show you the place and gone to grab Luke. The blame for this is on me. If I had been there for him, this wouldn't have happened."

"You don't know that."

Yeah, he did, because if he had been the one watching Luke and the twins, he would have never let those boys out of his sight. However, it hadn't been fucking Caleb on guard but Andrew. A man with no predator sense, an idiot who would probably die quickly if he had to survive in the wild. *Because I'd kill him.*

The weak bastard didn't pay attention to those he guarded. Andrew let himself be distracted.

Like I was distracted. Point the finger in the right place.

"This isn't your fault," Renny said, linking her fingers through his where they rested on the car's stick shift.

"Feels like it is."

"We might be worrying for nothing. Maybe Luke just wandered a little too far into the swamp while playing a game of hide-and-seek."

Since she didn't seem to believe her own reassurance, he chose to drive faster and soon drew the car up to the front of the Bittech building.

On the patterned cement outside the main doors, Melanie, with her hands latched to the twins, paced.

Relinquishing her grip on his hand, Renny barely waited for the car to stop before she was tumbling out. "What happened?"

"Andrew was around back with the boys. He says his phone rang, and he turned around to talk to whoever it was for only a second. Which is a second too long," Melanie grumbled. "He knows how quick the boys are. The next thing Andrew knew, the twins came screaming out of the woods, talking about the dino again."

"I might have to kill your husband," Caleb announced.

"Get in line." A scowl marred Melanie's features. "I already told him I'd yank his guts out if anything happens to Luke."

"I'll hold him down for you," Caleb offered.

"No need, Wes already offered."

"Where is Wes?" Renny asked, looking from side to side.

"Looking for Luke, of course."

"Andrew, too?"

Disdain wouldn't allow itself to be contained. Caleb snorted. "Doubtful."

Melanie's lips turned even lower. "He's inside calling some people to get a search party going."

"He's a bear. He should have been able to sniff out his trail." Renny took the words right out of his mouth.

If Caleb hadn't once seen Andrew's puny brown bear, he might have accused him of being a koala. Then again, that was insulting vicious koalas everywhere.

"Where was Luke last seen?" Caleb asked.

"By the willow tree that—Renny," Melanie

yelled. "Get your ass back here. You can't go rushing into the swamp like that. You're human. You won't be able to defend yourself."

The truth hit hard, and Renny stumbled to a halt. She whirled, tears streaming down her cheeks. The pure anguish she displayed was something Caleb well understood. Pain was a close companion, but he couldn't give in to his pain right now. Yes, he was chilled to the bone by what might be happening to his son. He was devastated he'd not protected Renny from this. But he was also calm and clearheaded. Not a single shake in his hands, his breathing regular.

Panic had no place right now. The man he used to be stood straight as Renny cried, "I don't care if I don't have a weapon. That's my son in there, and he needs me."

And Renny needed him. Caleb strode to her, making every effort to appear non-threatening, as he did not want her to bolt. Melanie was right. The swamp wouldn't prove kind to his delicate woman. Only the foolish—or desperate—went off into the swamp without a weapon or a plan.

Sensing she was ready to flee, he resorted to words since he wasn't in reach. "What happened to your theory that said he might be playing hide and go seek?"

"I lied. Something's wrong. I feel it, feel it in here." Renny thumped her stomach.

Funny how she pinpointed the spot he felt a twinge, too. The gut always knew.

"You're probably right. Things don't look too good,"—*Great pep talk so far. Why not make her face blanch further?*—"but I will promise you one thing." As he got close to her, he reached out to grasp her hand, giving it a squeeze. "I'll find him." *Fucking right I'll find him, even it's the last thing I do.*

"We'll find him."

He shook his head. "I can't risk you getting hurt. Melanie's right. How would you defend yourself? Make a slingshot out of your bra?" He forced a wan smile, but Renny simply stared at him. Eyes brimming, lips trembling.

Heartbreaking. *Fix this.*

With one last press of fingers, he let her go and went to walk past Renny. As if she'd let him go.

She grabbed his arm and held him until he faced her. "I have to go with you. He needs me."

"Duh, he needs you," Melanie said with a roll of her eyes. As they'd talked, she'd marched herself and the boys over. "You should go, but take this with you."

This being a gleaming gun, redolent with fresh oil, that Melanie pulled out of an oversized purse.

What was more disturbing? The fact that Melanie carried a loaded weapon along with a sealed container of green grapes or that Renny grabbed it, popped it open to take a peek at how it was loaded, then armed it. *Click.*

There went his argument and his resolve.

"Let's go," Renny said.

He might have argued, but Renny was armed with a gun and looked ready to use it. Was it worth wasting a breath asking her to stay with Melanie while he looked? Nope. She'd never listen, not with Luke in danger.

Just like he would never hold back.

"Try and keep up, baby." Caleb ran for the rear

of the building, outpacing Renny. His fingers—
perfectly steady and adept—slipped buttons from loops
and loosed his belt so that, when he hit the edge of the
swamp, he could shed that fabric layer and, in the
moment before he ducked under the concealing fronds
of the weeping willow, take his other shape.

No hesitation. Not this time.

A hunter was needed. A killer, too, because not
only was Caleb planning to return with his son, he was
also making sure the threat was eliminated once and for
all.

Skin stretched, limbs reshaped, and during the
process, he heard Renny's jogging steps, but he didn't
spare her a thought. Other things preoccupied his
mind.

As his claws dug into moist dirt, he opened all
his senses. His sensory spots absorbed and sifted the
very flavor of the air.

A vivid tableau comprised of scents was
painted. So many definite elements, layered and
interwoven among each other. Amongst the fetid
stench of the beast was the purer innocence of his son.
He smelled fear, the sharp acrid tang of a child
frightened.

The oddity, though, was how the smell of the
creature suddenly appeared. Caleb found no tracks to
show how it got there. Could locate no trail to follow,
and yet, the beast had been here, been here, and had
taken his son.

Maybe he'd missed something. He inhaled deep,
as deep as he could, and then sifted the results.

The odors of the swamp permeated the air,
nothing strange about that. However, he did note

another reptilian scent, a predator. Wes.

They went this way.

Not far, though. He could see where the footprints stopped. At the murky edge of the water.

Water that Renny shouldn't swim in, but she was beyond reason.

Intent on her goal—save Luke—she brushed past him and slogged in the liquid, arms above her head to keep the pistol dry, but vulnerable to anything that hid in the murky depths, and what about when they hit deeper water? How would she stay afloat or defend herself?

Yet he knew she'd never stay behind—not unless she was bound tight—and there wasn't a boat or anything she could use as a...

What of a raft?

He was horrified at the idea his croc projected, and had he been in charge, he might have vetoed it, but his beast was driving at the moment. His reptile floated alongside Renny, back straight and partially out of the water.

No way will my croc let Renny ride him. Nor should she. Forget the indignity, what if my beast gets hungry and thinks she'd make a nice treat?

The disgust his reptile radiated actually managed to shame him. In that one emotional outburst from his other half, Caleb had a shining moment where he understood something truly important. *My beast cares for them, too.*

Renny was *their* mate. Luke was *their* son.

Even cold-blooded predators didn't eat family. Okay, so maybe some did, but apparently no one ever proved that leaked cookbook belonged to the Mercers and that Aunt Tanya's rump roast was anything more than it seemed.

While Caleb grasped his croc's intent, Renny needed a minute or so to figure it out. It took a few bumps of his snout to snag her attention.

"What do you want?" she asked, looking quite cross.

The big reptile moved ahead then across, blocking her with his body.

"What are you doing, Cal?" She cocked her head while asking.

Cal? Had she finally chosen a nickname for him? Ugh, his croc grunted as a spurt of warmth made Caleb mentally grin.

Pay attention, his croc snapped.

His beast was right. He should exult in it later. Speed was of the essence, which meant Renny needed to get her ass on his back so he could get moving. By now, the thing that had taken his son could be anywhere.

But there is nowhere that can hide him.

I will find my son.

Another head butt against Renny and she thankfully grasped his plan. Reaching over him, she grabbed hold and heaved herself on. With one hand doing its best to grip, the other he assumed holding the gun since he could still smell the oil used to lubricate the metal, he set off on a glide.

Which direction, though?

The scent of the creature had disappeared at the water's edge. Had it dove? Fuck no, not with Luke in its grasp.

And it wasn't just fatherly hope that prayed

against that scenario. The evidence wasn't there. The rushes of weeds springing upward showed only one disturbance, and that one belonged exclusively to Wes, the lingering scent and disturbance of the fronds a message relayed to the sensory spots along his jaw.

Wes came through here, but the creature and Luke didn't.

But the footsteps ended at the water's edge. A body of water that held no trace of them. So where had they gone? There were no trees for them to climb, no signs of a boat or other floating device. A crazier man might wonder if they'd taken to the air. Impossible for a lizard.

Even one with possible wings? He couldn't help but recall that disturbing video.

If it can fly, though, then it could be anywhere. How could he track something that could take to the air currents and bypass all of the obstacles? Perhaps leave the swamp entirely.

"Where did it take Luke?" Renny murmured from his back. "How will we find him?"

The hopelessness in her tone crushed his heart.

I know where to go.

The man might wonder where to look, but his beast instinctively seemed to know.

Our son.

Did a link truly exist between him and Luke? Was that tickle he felt in his heart more than just trepidation?

Stop yapping or I'll eat something squishy. His croc threatened a mental image Caleb could have done without.

Powerful body undulating in the water, his croc

made toward the horizon, where an amber-red sun set. Funny how once his beast had chosen a direction, Caleb noted it was where the tug in his gut led.

It took his reptile and Renny over deep water, his large presence scattering those who feared becoming dinner.

Later. His croc grinned in the water, and Caleb groaned.

Must you do that?

I'm hungry was the snarky reply.

However much his beast side teased, he didn't delay and made a beeline—or should that be crocoline?—toward a rocky hillock, a bramble-covered thumb sticking out of the water.

Thorny Point, a place long avoided by children and adults alike because of the wicked barbed bushes. It had also been ignored by him and Wes during their search because it lacked the right kind of scent.

No scent usually meant no prey, so they never went ashore. But if the creature could fly? A glance upwards didn't reveal anything, but he still had to stop and take a look.

We might be wasting time.

But what if this is the place?

What if it's not?

He swam around the thrusting rocks, wondering if his gut led him astray. A good thing he stuck around, too, because what the senses didn't smell, the ears heard.

A whimper. A little boy whimper.

Luke!

An urgent need to get to the top of the islet imbued him, but first he had to dump a passenger. He maneuvered himself alongside a rock large enough for her to climb on. He didn't think she'd heard Luke— human hearing not being as developed—but she had a motherly instinct that sent her looking for handholds on the rocks and a path through the bushes.

Wait for me. A thought she didn't hear, and that meant he needed to quickly follow. Scrambling through the bramble in his bulky body would make too much noise, and climbing was easier when sporting fingers, which was why he took a moment to return to his human guise. And just in time, too, if he wanted to catch Renny, who'd scurried ahead of him.

At least she wore clothes. Caleb bit back curses as the thorns and prickly branches tore fine scratches along his skin while the moss-covered rocks slathered his skin in goo. But he didn't care about the minor irritations. Razor-sharp blades could have lined his path, and he would have still forged ahead.

His recklessness gave him speed, and he passed Renny, who'd finally paused to tuck the gun in the waistband of her pants. Hard to climb one-handed.

Reaching the top first, Caleb took a second to scan the area. He found himself in a small clearing, the ground hard and knotted, the bushes having been torn out, leaving behind uneven lumps. Within the created space, the reek of the creature permeated. Given the only tunnel in the brambled mess was the one Caleb had created, Caleb really believed his crazy theory that it might have flown had more weight.

During his quick evaluation of the area, a panting Renny had arrived and placed herself at his side. She didn't spare the spot more than a cursory glance. Upon spotting the shadowy crevice at the base of the jumble of rocks in the clearing, she immediately took a step toward it

Snagging her arm, Caleb halted her and shook his head. Putting a finger to his lips, he took the lead, ensuring his body provided a shield in the off chance something came rushing from the darkness of the cave.

After a few steps into the stony crevice, the sounds of the bayou faded, and the only things he could hear were the rasp of their feet on the ground and their breathing.

Noisy, but silence at this point wouldn't completely hide them. Air was being sucked into this cave, and as the current rushed past them, it pulled their scent with it. Surprise was out of the question, but he still tried to remain as stealthy as possible.

The military had taught him well when it came to stalking, a teaching forgotten at the whimpered, "Daddy?" It took Renny grasping his arm to prevent him from bolting ahead.

Only fools rushed in.

Or crazy fucking crocodiles. Snap. His reptile wiggled around inside, but Caleb paid him no mind as he reassessed.

Think with your head, not your heart. Because his head would hopefully keep them all alive.

The tremulous query came from around the bend, a bend he could see because of a faint orange illumination. As he slid around the curve, blind to whatever hid behind it, he held himself ready, still in his human guise. This confined space wasn't made for a croc to fight.

Put him in the water and he would clamp his jaws, grab with claws, and roll with the bastard. On dry land, even worse in a tight cave, his beast would be at a disadvantage.

Good thing he had more skills than just a pair of powerful jaws for snapping. He clenched his fists, and as he fully came around the rocky bend, instinct ensured he was just in time to block the blow aimed at his face.

A fetid whiff of the creature enveloped him.

Found you.

And the monster wasn't happy about that. The impact of the punch against Caleb's forearm forced a grunt from him.

The fucker is strong.

And by strong, he meant a seven-footish, hulking green lizard man with linebacker-wide-plus-some shoulders and a vile smile distorted by the teeth-filled beak.

"Well, aren't you a cute specimen? Not," Caleb taunted as he braced against another blow then jabbed out. His shot connected…with a slab-like chin.

Ouch.

"Is your face made of bloody rock?"

The thing hissed at him and jabbed its tongue. Caleb tilted his head to the side, but didn't quite escape the wet drool.

"Gross, dude." More than disgusting, poisonous.

Caleb would have cursed his stupidity in not suspecting it except he felt himself fading fast. While shifters had a stronger-than-human ability to process drugs, it sometimes took several exposures to build an immunity.

Having never been licked by a mutant lizard

before, Caleb proved quite susceptible. And he saw rainbows, but that might have been an old concussion talking as a fist took him in the jaw.

Reeling on his feet, blinking past the rainbows, Caleb sought to regain control.

Must take out this threat before passing out. Caleb swung, but his movements were sluggish. Laughable even.

A granite fist caught him again on the jaw. A jab smacked him in the stomach.

Damn his uncooperative limbs!

Within the space of a blink, Caleb found himself on his knees.

Little hands grabbed at him, and he saw the wavering shape of his son's face.

"Daddy!"

"Caleb."

Two voices yelling for him and he couldn't make his thick tongue answer. All Caleb could do was look up at the reptilian creature that had taken him down with mere spit.

The indignity of it.

The shame... His croc rolled and rolled in a deathly parody in his head.

Asshole.

Who will save our woman and son?

Who, indeed, if Caleb was taken out?

You are not alone.

He didn't have to be a hero today. The important thing was that they survived. And with that thought, he managed to focus enough to blurt out the words, "Shoot it, baby."

Chapter Eighteen

Shoot it?

Big blue eyes stared at Renny. Human eyes in the face of a monster.

The gun trembled in her hand, her outstretched arms, feeling the pressure to remain steady, to keep her aim true.

Renny knew how to fire a pistol, smaller pistols than the one she held, but same concept. Aim. Shoot. But this wasn't a paper target or a pop can. *It's alive.* Could she really kill the creature in front of her? *Is it even a creature? I would swear it's a shifter of some kind.* One with too many different parts.

As if sensing her wavering resolve, the lizard beast reached out a hand, misshapen with some fingers and claws, a mash-up of human and reptile. "Nnnnno."

The word shocked her, reaffirming the belief that this was more than just a creature. Was this thing before her the result of a shift gone wrong?

To the side of the upright reptile, where Caleb lay still, his eyes shuttered, Luke crouched. A gaze filled with moisture, he said in a tremulous voice, "Mommy. I'm scared."

So was she, dammit, but could she shoot the thing with human eyes in front of her? What if this was a misunderstanding?

She tried reason first. "Listen, I don't know who

you are"—or what—"but I don't want to hurt you. I just want my son back."

The thing cocked its head. It made an odd sound, a cross between a cluck and a purr.

"I can tell there's someone in there." Perhaps not a sane person, given the flat chill in the eyes. "And I'm sure you have a reason why you took Luke. Perhaps you thought you were protecting him."

"He's bad, Mommy," Luke cried out.

This outburst agitated the creature, and it whipped its head sideways to emit a baleful hiss. It also flicked its sinuous, scale-covered tail.

The tip of it swept across the floor in its agitation, knocking something loose from an alcove in the wall. A rock rolled and bounced, stopping at Renny's feet.

Except it wasn't a rock.

A perfect little skull stared up at her. A child's skull.

This isn't a human. It's a monster. Now Renny was the one with cold running through her veins as she steadied her arm. The creature read her intent and lunged as she fired—*Bang!*—and managed to miss! Unused to a gun of this caliber, Renny didn't expect the recoil that threw off her aim. It proved a costly mistake.

The lizard thing hit her and took her to the ground hard.

"Ah!" Renny managed a short scream and stared in wide-eyed horror at the reptilian face above hers, the jaws cracked open wide, the venom dripping from its fangs.

Struggling with the body pinning her did nothing. It outweighed her too much to even rock it.

"Let go of my mommy!" Luke cried.

Oh God, her little boy. Even as her hands scrambled to hold back the nightmare visage, she screamed, "Run, Luke. Run and find help!"

The strength of the creature was frightening. It barely seemed to make an effort, and yet it pushed toward her face as if she didn't hold it back at all. Fetid breath washed over her. Those big blue eyes didn't bother to hide their malevolence.

She closed her eyes tight lest she witness her own death.

Only death didn't come. Rescue did.

"Like fuck. Get your slimy green ass off my baby!" Caleb roared.

Opening her eyes, Renny was just in time to see the body of the creature get plucked and tossed.

The lizard hit the wall hard, but that didn't stop it. Hitting the ground, it sprang to its feet, its forked tongue flicking.

"Food plays? Fun." The grotesque words emerged on a sibilant hiss.

"It's a shifter," Renny breathed, unable to hide her horror.

"It's an abomination," Caleb growled, standing between Renny and the beast.

Just in time, too, as the monster dove at Caleb, and the next thing she knew, they were wrestling, the muscles in Caleb's biceps bulging as he fought to hold the fury of the creature back.

"Get out of here, baby," he grunted, his words so reminiscent of what she'd told Luke. But just like Luke had lingered, so would she. Caleb had made a vow to never let her down, to always protect her, and

211

she loved him enough to do the same.

Since Luke had tucked himself out of sight around the corner, she didn't waste time looking for him. She hit the ground on hands and knees, the faint illumination from an electrical lantern causing more shadows than revelations. She looked for the gun she'd lost as grunts and thuds sounded, the battle between man and lizard happening in earnest.

But a man couldn't hope to hold against a monster.

"Argh."

She turned her head in time to see the injury. A swipe of a claw across Caleb's shoulder saw blood streaming, bright red against his skin, the coppery tang filling the air.

The monster gurgled in triumph, and Caleb stumbled back, head shaking as if dazed. "Don't let is scratch you," he warned, his words slurred. "Poison on its claws and saliva."

Dropping to his knees, Caleb blinked as he tried to fight the effects of the drug. The creature let out a warble, took a step forward, and lifted its arm, claws extended, ready to swipe.

"Caleb!" she cried. No. This couldn't be happening. They'd just found each other again.

I can't lose him.

Cold metal met her fingers, and she spared a quick glance down to see Luke had found the gun and placed it in her hand. She didn't need his solemn gaze to know what had to be done.

"Die!" Renny screamed the word as she fired the weapon, this time holding it with both hands, but even then, the recoil screwed with her, and she hit the lizard in the shoulder. Missed. Fire again. Hit. The lower belly.

Then it was on her, and it was all she could do to avoid its wide-open jaws. Luckily, it wasn't drooling hard enough to poison her. On the contrary, it seemed to be most careful that she remained conscious for its pleasure.

"Eat you alive." The sibilant words brought her level of terror to a whole new level.

Renny heard screaming—hers, Luke's, hers again. And then she went silent, her cry lost at the sight of Caleb, but a Caleb like she'd never seen. Half-man, half-croc, big, muscled and oh so very pissed. Caleb loomed, and in this hybrid shape, in fury and size, he was more than a match for the monster.

With webbed fingers, tipped in claws, Caleb grabbed the thing and lifted it. Tossed it. It hit the wall and rose, just like before. However, this time, her half-shifted lover was there to greet it.

"Don't. Hurt. My Family!" Caleb managed to spit the words out of a less-than-human mouth filled with teeth as he grappled the thing into submission.

He wrapped a thickly muscled forearm around its neck and squeezed. Squeezed tight enough that those blue eyes widened. The mouth, lined with venomous teeth, gaped as it gasped for air.

But Caleb didn't relent. He kept applying pressure until the light in those uncanny blue eyes faded. The body went limp. He held on a while longer, but there wasn't a single twitch.

Caleb released the creature, but when Renny would have run to him, he held up a scaled hand and said, "Don't. I'm not myself. I don't want to hurt you."

While more guttural than usual, she had no problem understanding his words. She just didn't agree with them.

What a load of... "Bullshit." Renny said the word and smiled at the shock in his eyes. No matter what shape he wore, she knew those eyes. Just like she knew him. "You would never hurt me. Never hurt us," she amended as Luke threw himself at Caleb.

Still in his half-shape, Caleb caught the little body and held his son gently against him.

Renny approached and placed a hand on his chest, not caring if it was covered in scales. Not caring if, right now, Caleb was caught between two worlds, man and beast. This was who he was, and he needed to know that.

"I love you, Caleb."

"Me, too!" Luke piped in. "Daddy killed the dinosaur."

Or not. Renny screamed as a hand closed around her ankle, the sharp points of the claws digging into her boots.

Bang.

"Stubborn fucker. Heal from that," Wes snapped. Turning his gaze on Caleb, Wes smirked. "Dude, put some fucking clothes on. No one needs to see your shriveled green lizard."

Caleb glared, and Renny probably didn't help the situation by bursting into giggles.

Chapter Nineteen

The burning scowl Caleb turned Wes's way didn't deter the other man from giving a sneered, "You're welcome. Looks like I got here just in time."

"I had things under control," Caleb managed to say through his strangely shaped jaw. Weird didn't begin to describe his partial shift, a shift he was losing his hold on as his adrenaline dissipated.

Renny stepped away, Luke cradled in her arms, a situation his son was not happy about it.

"Put me down. I'm not a baby," Luke protested.

If his jaw wasn't in the process of realigning itself, Caleb might have laughed at her indignant look.

Ignoring them all, Wes knelt by the monster's corpse. "Well, this is fucking interesting," Wes muttered as Caleb's last joint popped back into its human shape.

"What did you find?" Renny asked, crouching down to look at what held Wes's interest.

The other man held up the mottled arm of the dead creature. Even through the scaling and discoloration, Caleb noted the tattoo.

"Recognize it?" Caleb asked.

"No, but then again, I don't go around cataloguing people's tats."

"Hold on a second," Renny said with a frown. "I thought shifters couldn't do tattoos, something about your skin rejecting the ink."

"Natural-born shifters can't have them, but someone who was turned with one already..." Wes shrugged. "Possible, I guess. I don't know too many converts, though, so I couldn't say for sure."

"If this guy was intentionally changed, who did it? And what?" Even with all Caleb had seen, he'd never come across anything like it. "I've never heard or seen anything like it."

"Me either. And it doesn't smell right," Wes mumbled, reiterating the problem Caleb had since their first encounter with the thing.

"It's like a mishmash of stuff I know, with something else thrown into the mix."

Wes looked up at him. "Yup. And look at this." This time, their attention was drawn to the neck of the creature, where singed flesh formed a ring.

"What the hell would do that?"

"Makes me think of a shock collar," Renny observed.

Which only served to deepen the mystery.

What also proved complicated? Getting them all back to dry land. Lucky for them, Wes had a weatherproof bag he'd brought along on the hunt—*"A must have for all swamp predators so they don't get caught out in the open with no underwear."* He also had a phone.

It wasn't long before they were back on dry land, Bittech property to be exact, inside one of the docking bays, shifters of all castes called in for the search and eventual rescue gathered around the corpse of the lizard thing.

While everyone stared, eyes wide with confusion and shock, only a few whispers were uttered.

"Who was it?" No one seemed to recognize the body or the tattoo.

"What is it?" The hybrid mix was not something anyone ever recalled seeing or hearing about.

"Who did this?" The question that haunted them most of all.

Who would do such a thing? And why?

Bittech claimed no knowledge of the creature, and despite Wes's suspicions, Caleb had seen Andrew's face. Either the man was an excellent actor or he'd never seen the monster before. No one could fake the revulsion on his face.

Yet, the fact remained, this thing wasn't naturally born. It had been made.

A mystery that would require solving, but not tonight. Tonight, Caleb took his family home. Not the new one with its bare rooms, but his childhood home, where he knew they would all feel safe.

Constantine, who it turned out had done his fair share of searching but in another direction of the swamp, had arrived before them. He sat on the couch, freshly showered, with his dog sleeping on his lap. Or not.

Princess opened a single eye, just a slit, and the corner of her mouth lifted. Her canine version of hello or the one he suspected of meaning, "I've got my eye on you."

As Renny bathed Luke, Caleb hit the outdoor shower unit to sluice the bayou from his skin. Rinsing it, though, didn't help him from reliving the moment in the cave when he'd thought the creature would kill Renny.

This finally brought on the shakes. He dropped

to his knees as the realization he could have lost Renny and Luke truly hit him.

So close, so close to losing to that monster.

He'd known he couldn't fight the beast as a man, and his croc knew that it wasn't the right weapon either, but when they decided to partner together… Together they formed an incredible duo. For the first time, they'd truly shared everything—body and mind.

And he hadn't eaten anybody. *Score!* Except now he was kind of hungry.

Feed me. Lots of fish in the bayou. Crunch. Crunch.

Sometimes I'm really tempted to see you made into a purse.

But their banter wasn't acerbic in nature. Caleb finally understood his croc's cold sense of humor, and he now knew he could trust it.

Trust himself.

To placate them both, he made himself the thickest roast beef sandwich ever using the reddest parts he could find.

Compromise, the key to living in harmony with himself.

A clean Luke was spat out from the bathroom, dressed in clean pajamas with dogs on them—sigh—and wet hair. "Watch him, would you, while I shower?"

Seemed simple enough. Caleb swung his son into his arms and carried him to his room. He tucked him in bed, worried at how quiet his boy was, but at a loss as to what to do. He pulled a book from the nightstand, something with a happy title and happy cartoon faces, but he hesitated.

He put the book aside and paced. "Your mom should be out of the shower any second now." She would know what to do. The right thing to say. *But I'm his father. I should know how to handle this.*

"Do you need anything?"

Luke gave a slow shake of his head, then his mini me peered up at him, and the surge of love for this child—*my son*—took Caleb to his knees so he could meet Luke's gaze without making him crane.

"Are you all right?" Caleb asked, knowing all too well how some events could mark a man and weaken him. Except…he'd not caved to weakness or anxiety. Not this time. As a matter of fact, Caleb realized he'd not felt that debilitating panic hardly at all in the last week. And since Renny had slept with him, he'd not needed his pills because being with her held the nightmares at bay.

She's better than any head shrink or drug.

"I was scared," his son admitted, his chin drooping. "I'm sorry."

"Don't you dare apologize," Caleb admonished. "Fear is normal. Hell, don't tell anyone"—he lowered his voice—"but I was pretty scared, too. That was one scary dude."

"He's gone though, right?" Uncertainty wavered in his son's eyes.

Yes, but the mystery remained of where it had come from. However, he wasn't about to worry his son further. Caleb gave him the reassurance he needed. "That monster isn't coming back."

"Even if it did," Renny said, stepping into the bedroom, "Daddy would take care of it."

At her certainty, his chest swelled. "Always," he promised. "I will always be there for you." He whispered those words to Luke as he kissed him on the forehead, tucking him in for the night. Nothing could ever tear him from those who needed him. Who loved him.

As Caleb rose and readied to leave, Renny hesitated. "Maybe I should stay with him."

And maybe Caleb needed to put a bell on a certain mutt because Princess suddenly scooted through his legs, startling the fuck out of him before she hopped onto the bed, did a circle, and lay down, tucked against Luke. His son reached out a hand to stroke the dog.

"Go, Mommy. I'm not a baby. 'Sides, Princess is here, and she's a good guard dog."

Freaky dog more like it, given he could have sworn Princess winked.

Shutting the door, he and Renny made their way to the living room, only to notice Constantine still hogged the couch.

"I can't wait to move into the new place," Caleb said with a sigh.

His brother snorted. "That makes two of us then. But until that happens, which is tomorrow, by the way, because I've taken the day off to move your shit, you guys can borrow my room. You know, so you can have some privacy."

"Really?" Caleb couldn't help his surprised query.

"Yeah, really. You might still be an asshole, but you're my brother, and you've had a rough night. You both have, so take my room for the night, but you'd better strip those sheets in the morning," Constantine muttered as Caleb, not wasting any time, grabbed Renny around the waist and carted her back down the hall.

She giggled as he closed the door and leaned on it. "That was kind of rude."

"No, rude would have been kicking him off the couch to make out with you."

"And is that what we're going to do? Make out?"

"For starters," he said with a grin.

Her teasing lilt faded as she asked, "Do you think it's over?"

He hoped so. "Unless there's another one of those mutants running about, then yeah."

"Who would create such a thing, and why?"

He shrugged. "I don't know. Maybe we're wrong. We can't know for sure anyone made it." Something he didn't entirely believe, but he sensed she needed reassurance. Hell, so did he. "The world is a big fucking place with lots of secrets."

"Except between us." She caught his gaze. "I saw you tonight, Caleb. Saw you. Saw your croc. Saw what you could do."

As she spoke, his body tensed, fear coiling in him. Was this where she finally realized she couldn't handle him?

"You took care of me, and our son. I know you were scared of letting the beast out, but..." She took a step toward him and cupped his face. "Even when you change, you're still you. Still my Caleb."

"A man capable of killing."

"A man who will protect us with everything he's got." She leaned close and kissed him. "A man I love." In a flash, he bound her so tightly she laughed even as she gasped. "Caleb!"

He loosened his grip, just a little, and buried his face in her hair. "I love you, too, baby. So fucking much it scares me. I lost you once to the croc inside me—"

She shook her head. "No, you lost me once because people wanted to use the beast inside you. But we're smarter now. We won't ever let that happen again."

"Never." A promise he sealed with a kiss, a kiss that started out soft and sweet.

However, Renny didn't want gentle, or so he surmised as her teeth nipped at his lower lip. Her mouth left his mouth to travel the length of his stubbled jaw, moving down the column of his throat and pausing over his pulse. She sucked at it, a seemingly innocent gesture that meant a lot to his kind. Letting someone close to a jugular was the ultimate trust.

She kept sucking as her hands tugged at his shirt. He helped her to strip it from his body. He couldn't help but lean against the wall as her lips continued their exploration, burning-hot touches across his upper body. A bite of his nipples. A raking of her nails down his chest to the waistband of his athletic pants.

As she knelt, she yanked at them, baring his erect shaft and pulling a, "What are you doing?" question from him.

The smile that curved her lips went well with the teasing glint in her eye. "Take a guess."

Why guess when she showed him?

"Baby…" He whispered the word as she drew him into her mouth and proceeded to blow him.

Literally.

Chapter Twenty

Funny how surviving what seemed like certain death left a woman feeling more alive than ever. Or was it the man standing before her that had brought her back to life?

They'd both gone through so much. Pain, betrayal, heartache. But now that the secrets were exposed, apologies made, and love rekindled, there was nothing keeping them apart.

Nothing to stop her from showing Caleb her love—and affection.

There was also nothing stopping her from showing him how much she appreciated him, loved him.

She took him into her mouth, the velvety skin of his shaft a sensory delight to explore. While thick, she could accommodate him by stretching her mouth wide. Even then, her teeth grazed him, a sensation he enjoyed if his shivers were anything to judge by.

She dug her fingers into his hips, giving herself leverage to bob her head back and forth along the length of him, savoring every hard inch. Loving how he pulsed and even twitched in her mouth.

The soft moans let her know he was lost in the moment, but she wanted more than that. She wanted him to lose control. To lose himself in her.

She worked him with her mouth, her tongue

dancing patterns on his skin, her lips suctioning his plump head. She suctioned hard, willing him to come, but Caleb had other ideas.

"You're driving me wild," he growled as he pulled her to her feet. But she didn't remain on her feet long. In a whirl of bodies, he had her pinned against the wall, suspended by the sheer strength in his hands.

"I love you," she murmured. Loved his strength, all of him.

"And I," he whispered back as the tip of him entered her, "have always." Thrust. "Loved." Deep grind. "You." With that last word, he claimed her mouth, even as his cock claimed her pussy.

He pounded into her, stretching her with his size, reaching deep within and touching more than her G-spot. He touched her soul.

Together, they panted and thrust in and against each other, together racing for the pinnacle of bliss.

When she would have cried out, he caught her lips, not only swallowing her expression of pleasure, but she reveled in every single quiver of his body, and then his own unrestrained cry as he orgasmed and brought her with him.

Together, they rode the wild storm of their love and emerged from it breathless, dewy, and smiling.

But she did have to wonder, "Why are you laughing?"

"Because for the first time since I got back, we had access to a perfectly fine bed, and yet we didn't even come close to using it."

She smiled. "Seems a shame to waste it, unless you're too tired."

Her teasing dare bore fruit. And later on, nestled

in his arms, she couldn't help but murmur, "I'm glad you returned."

"So am I. And I'm never leaving again."

But they would be investing in a lock, given Luke's exclamation the following morning of, "Mommy, you forgot to put on pajamas!"

Epilogue

The dinosaur sightings stopped the night they killed the monster, as did the disappearances, but the bodies of those missing were never found. Five in all and none of them the remains left behind in the cave.

Actually, the Bittech lab tests showed the skeletons found, eight that they could be sure of, were all several years old. It closed a few cold cases and made many wonder just how long the dino creature had lived there undetected.

As no one could come up with answers, the curious went back to their lives, even Wes, because no matter how much he and Caleb, along with the others, searched, they could find no wrongdoing by Bittech or any of its employees. Their paranoia proved groundless, but Wes refused to give up.

"I'm telling you there's something fishy going on."

Caleb didn't disagree, but without a trail, or any clues, there wasn't much he could do other than promise his aid should Wes discover something. In the meantime, while they waited to see if life would stay normal, he had a family that needed him.

Although it had been only a few weeks since Caleb's return, life had changed drastically. All for the better.

With the house Caleb had scored meeting approval from Renny and Luke, she'd given her notice to the guy she rented her apartment from, and they were already moved in. Even better, with Caleb's mom quitting her job to become a full-time grandmother and babysitter for her grandson, it meant Renny could stick to one job, part-time. He wasn't crazy about her choice of remaining as a waitress for the Itty Bitty Club, but she was working the day shift now and home before dark. While he might not like her job, his best friend Daryl loved it because Renny made sure he got the employee discount on drinks, which meant more tips for everyone since Daryl spent most of his lunches there.

Goddamned perv. But Caleb loved the guy, so he tolerated it.

Life was fucking sweet. He was in love. Had a son. A job.

As for his croc, since their recent understanding, Caleb found he didn't resent it, but then again, he also made sure to let it out as often as he could. In return, his reptile slumbered more peacefully in his mind, and while it didn't give up hunting entirely, at least Caleb could content himself that the prey they hunted wasn't human.

And he felt more human than he had in years.

Except when the football hit him in the head, and Daryl laughed. Then he chased the damned cat, who was nimble no matter his form, up a tree while his son cheered him on and Renny clapped.

Life was fucking grand—*and we'll eat anyone who tries to mess it up.*

Snap.

*

Well, this didn't bode well. Finding oneself tied to a chair, fully clothed and alone, was never a good sign. Naked and with a lady friend? Totally another thing.

But nope, no hottie in a latex suit. No feathers for tickling. Yet Daryl was definitely bound and a prisoner.

There was a light somewhere behind him, probably a lamp, given it didn't come from overhead. It provided enough illumination to see his odd situation. Seated in a straight-back, metal-framed chair with a plastic bucket to cradle his large frame. The kind of chair you saw in cafeterias and, judging by the wobble when he swished his hips, not too solid.

That's method number one to escape.

Two was snapping the tape that bound him to the chair. A simple twist of his large upper body should do it.

Onto the third item, what of his hands? Those were, surprisingly enough, taped in front of him.

By whom, fucking amateurs? Don't they know how dangerous I am?

Who the hell secured a dangerous predator with their hands in front of them? Because, seriously, if there was anyone dangerous, it was Daryl.

Not conceit, simple fact.

Daryl tested the tape binding his wrists together. He didn't break it right away. Never act too hasty, not if one wanted the element of surprise. But he almost forgot his own rule when he noted the duct tape was patterned with ducks.

What the hell?

He peered down, and sure enough, more of the happy yellow rubber duckies swam across his chest across the tape layered there.

Mmm…duck. His feline did so enjoy a well-roasted one.

Apart from feeling a little peckish, Daryl was wondering if this was a joke. After all, this was the least intimidating abduction he'd ever heard of. When he recounted this story to his buds, he'd have to make sure he changed the ducks to sharks. Because at least they had big teeth. Or maybe he'd tell them he'd broken out of chains.

Yeah, big silver chains. That would impress them.

The dim light barely illuminated the place. Probably a good thing, given he was pretty sure the pink carpet, worn smooth in spots, was a relic from the nineties while the television, in its big hulking case, should have collapsed the dresser.

A classy motel, probably on the side of the highway somewhere, used as a quick pit stop by truckers and those looking for a place to wash and rest on a journey to somewhere.

But how did I get here?

That was the question because last he recalled, he was chatting with that lovely cocoa-skinned woman—and he meant *woman,* with curves that would spill over his palms, luscious lips that would look perfect about waist-height, and dark curly hair that spilled over her shoulders.

Hair that I wanted to pull, which was why I asked her if she wanted to go somewhere quieter.

To his surprise, she'd readily agreed, and they went outside. Whereupon she fucking stabbed him with a needle!

So was it any wonder when she walked in, not even two seconds after his recollection, that he blurted out, "You're the bitch who drugged me." And despite what she'd done, he still found her freaking hot, even if she did have a gun pointed at his face.

"Keep talking, darlin'. You're making my finger awfully twitchy." She canted her head to the side and smiled.

"I've got something that will fix that." And, yes, he made sure she got what he meant with a wink.

What he didn't expect was that she would laugh and say, "Oh, darlin', you wish you were man enough to handle me."

A dare? How he loved a challenge. His inner kitty twitched its tail in excitement. "You probably shouldn't have said that." He held her gaze and smiled as he snapped the tape holding his hands. His lips quirked as he stood with the chair and flexed, freeing himself and sending it crashing to the floor.

His sexy kidnapper slowly backed away, the gun never wavering, a touch of fear finally sparking in her eyes. But not enough to worry him, not when he could sense her skin heating as well.

"I'll give you a five-second head start," he offered.

Because his cat did so love a chase.

Growrrr.

Instead of bolting, though, she pulled the trigger at almost point-blank range.

But be sure to check out the next story, featuring Daryl: *A Panther's Claim.*

The End...for now.

Author Bio

Hello and thank you so much for reading my story. I

hope I kept you well entertained. As you might have noticed, I enjoy blending humor in to my romance. If you like my style then I have many other wicked stories that might intrigue you. Skip ahead for a sneak peek, or pay me a visit at http://www.EveLanglais.com

This Canadian author and mom of three would love to hear from you so be sure to connect with me.

Facebook: http://bit.ly/faceevel
Twitter: @evelanglais
Goodreads: http://bit.ly/evelgood
Amazon: http://bit.ly/evelamz
Newsletter: http://evelanglais.com/newrelease

CPSIA information can be obtained at www.ICGtesting.com
Printed in the USA
LVOW12s2206010316

477382LV00005B/169/P